JOHNNY ORTIZ: He's the half-Apache cop who's holding off a major Eastern crime syndicate from a rich new vein in an ugly trade. And he's not about to back down . . .

CASSIE ENRIGHT: A brilliant anthropologist and Johnny's *querida*, she's as fiercely committed to him as she is to her beloved desert land. The big-money men call that land real estate—and they're going to use Cassie to get it . . .

PAUL HARPER: Educated and handsome, the Eastern developer is a suspect—and tough competition for a local detective who's seen too much and loves too hard . . .

MARÍA VICTORIA SANCHEZ: She was a barrio girl who had to grow up fast. Now she's a woman who's risking her life to avenge her dead lover . . .

PETER ROSS: He's East Coast power, money and class, a devoted family man on vacation in Santo Cristo. But behind the facade are a thousand needlefuls of death. It's up to Ortiz to decide if he wants to play Ross as enemy—or ally . . .

"Johnny Ortiz is a welcome addition to the lists of the great detectives."

—Hillary Waugh

SANTO CRISTO IS A SMALL TOWN
EXPLODING IN BIG-TIME
GREED . . .

Books by Richard Martin Stern

Death in the Snow
Murder in the Walls
You Don't Need an Enemy

Published by POCKET BOOKS

Most Pocket Books are available at special quantity discounts for bulk purchases for sales promotions, premiums or fund raising. Special books or book excerpts can also be created to fit specific needs.

For details write the office of the Vice President of Special Markets, Pocket Books, 1230 Avenue of the Americas, New York, New York 10020.

DEATH
IN THE SNOW

Richard
Martin
Stern

POCKET BOOKS

New York   London   Toronto   Sydney   Tokyo

POCKET BOOKS, a division of Simon & Schuster Inc.
1230 Avenue of the Americas, New York, NY 10020

Copyright © 1973 by Richard Martin Stern
Cover art copyright © 1989 Joseph Cellini

Published by arrangement with the author
Library of Congress Catalog Card Number: 72-7731

ISBN: 0-671-65259-1

First Pocket Books printing October 1989

10 9 8 7 6 5 4 3 2 1

POCKET and colophon are trademarks of
Simon & Schuster Inc.

Printed in the U.S.A.

For D A S and E E V

DEATH
IN THE SNOW

—————— 1 ——————

The chinook wind is warm and dry, greedy; and it can come, as it came that March morning, out of a clear blue sky. The Blackfoot name for the wind is snow-eater. The name is apt.

In the great mountains behind the city of Santo Cristo, for months above the 10,000-foot contour the skiing had been good-to-excellent. Now within hours rocks and stumps began to show, and even in spots bare patches of earth where the snow cover had evaporated. Something else appeared, too, and it was Pete Tomlin, on ski patrol, who found it.

Pete was nineteen, a freshman at State U, home on spring vacation. He was a solid, well-built, well-coordinated, usually unflappable boy. No longer. "I'll tell you," he said frankly, "I'm shook." This was down at the ski lodge while they awaited the arrival of Authority. "What I saw first," Pete said, "was a rock, or maybe part of a tree stump sticking up." He shook his head. "It wasn't. It was a shoe. With a foot in it."

One of the Martin girls said incredulously, "You didn't touch it!"

Pete had. It hadn't looked like a skiing accident, and it wasn't; but if you were on ski patrol, it was up to you to investigate. "I don't know who he is," Pete said. "I never saw him before." He paused, and swallowed, remembering. "It looks like he's been there all winter."

Johnny Ortiz—Lieutenant Juan Felipe Ortiz, Santo Cristo Police—left his pick-up truck down at the Lodge, trudged up the slope beneath the ski lift, had his long look, and trudged back down again. His shoes and trouser legs almost to his knees were soaked; he ignored them. "Bring him down," he said. "I'll take him into town." For Doc Easy's examination; the body to the doctor, not vice versa. Doc was pushing seventy, a flatland easterner, and clambering around in snow above the 10,000-foot contour was not for him.

Sleds they had for skiing accidents. Three ski patrolmen rode the lift up to ski down with a sled and pick up the dead man.

Johnny sat in a corner of the big Lodge room with Pete Tomlin. "You found him."

"Yes, sir."

"Did you move him?"

It was disconcerting, Pete thought, because although he hadn't done a thing wrong, and knew it, still he was underage and fuzz were always to be viewed with suspicion if not distrust, and, besides, this Johnny Ortiz was a kind of local legend, part Anglo, part Spanish, part Apache, and when he turned those dark eyes on you, you began remembering all the tales you'd ever heard about scalping knives, and people staked out on ant hills. "I didn't, you know, *move* him," Pete said. "I brushed the snow away." And he couldn't help adding, "Was that wrong?"

Johnny's face softened a little. "The only way I can see you'd know what was there," he said. "Did you take anything?"

"No, sir."

"You're sure?"

"Yes, sir. I wouldn't—I mean, you know—" Pete was silent. Then, "Why? I mean, you know, is something gone?"

"He isn't wearing a belt," Johnny said.

Pete shook his head. "I didn't notice."

"And his pants are pretty loose around the middle." Johnny believed the boy, but the facts were there to be looked at. "And there he is, half mile from the nearest road. Do you suppose he walked, holding his pants up with one hand?" He made a small gesture of dismissal. "You don't know the answer," he said. "Neither do I." He paused. "And you don't know the man, do you?"

"No, sir." Pete swallowed. "Do you?"

"Not yet," Johnny said. He stood up, middle-sized, lean, wiry. "Thanks."

In the ski shop they kept snow records of a sort. Johnny studied them. "The first good snowfall was in December," he said, and Karl Utter, head ski instructor, agreed.

Perhaps half a meter," Karl said. He shrugged and smiled faintly. "Always we think, we hope for good

snow by the end of November, your Thanksgiving.''
The last word was difficult, the ksg came out gzz. "Almost always,'' he said, "we are disappointed. December, if we are lucky. Sometimes not good snow until January. This year, by the end of December we had a fair base, half a meter, maybe seventy centimeters. Then here," he touched the chart, "January, the first week, we had three days of snow. Since then, our base has not been less than a meter,'' he shook his head, unsmiling now, "until this wind, this *verdamnte* chinook. It does not melt the snow. It—how do you say?— sublimates it. You can almost see the snow disappearing, but there is no melting.'' He waved one hand in the air. "Poof! The snow is gone with the thirsty wind."

"Half a meter,'' Johnny said, "nineteen inches, twenty inches back in early December. Enough to cover a man?''

Karl thought about it. "I think not. Where he was, in the open, with wind sometimes blowing, I do not think so. A—mound one could see—'' He shook his head.

"But if he fell in the snow,'' Johnny said, "and was lying there when this January storm began?''

Karl nodded. "Then until today he would not be seen. Except by an accident.''

Johnny's eyebrows rose. "What kind of accident?''

"A bad fall, someone out of control, digging into that spot deep with his skis, his poles.'' Karl shrugged.

Johnny hadn't even thought about it, but there it was. "So since January probably,'' he said, "people have been skiing right over the top of him, is that it?''

Karl nodded. "That is so,'' he said.

* * *

Johnny drove down the mountainside neither fast nor slow. The body, wrapped in a ground sheet Karl Utter had lent, shared the truck bed with a shovel, a box of sand, and a tow cable, standard winter gear. In the rack across the rear window of the pick-up cab, Johnny's rifle rested securely, standard year-round fixture.

The road was dirt, graded fall and spring, snow-plowed at need. Upward-bound automobiles scrambling for traction during the winter had worn corrugations, and over these the pick-up bounced and jostled, and so did its load. If he had thought about it, which he did not, Johnny would have found nothing callous or even distasteful about a jostling corpse. When you were dead, you were dead; the spirit was gone, and what remained was without much importance—except for what it might be able to tell about the manner of its death.

He drove straight to the hospital, the pick-up's heavy snow tires humming a dirge on the dry city streets. Doc Easy was waiting, and two orderlies to unload the body. "He's been in cold storage," Johnny said, "and I don't suppose that's going to make things any easier for you, but anything you can tell us may help. We'll send his clothes over to Saul Pentland at State Police lab."

Doc said, "He's not exactly dressed for climbing around a ski slope in snow."

True enough; the body wore a dark suit, striped shirt and tie, black shoes, and a light raincoat, city wear.

"And," Doc said, "no belt." He lifted the waistband of the trousers; the waist was far from a snug fit. Doc looked at Johnny.

Johnny nodded. "They wouldn't stay up by them-selves. And why are they that loose anyway?" He shook his head. "See you, Doc."

He drove the pick-up back to headquarters and walked unhurriedly around to Al Packer's shop on the plaza. Al was a licensed Indian trader, and his shop specialized in Indian silverwork and blankets. "One of those fancy belts," Johnny said. "Silver and turquoise buckle and tip and those other things—"

"Keepers." Al nodded. "What about them?"

"Expensive?"

Al shrugged and smiled.

"I'm not out to buy," Johnny said. "I just want in-formation. How much, tops?"

Al shrugged again. "Maybe two hundred dollars," he said; and Johnny thought about it. Enough to tempt someone to violence? Maybe, maybe not, but somehow the picture was all wrong anyway: the dead man wore dude's clothing, and the kind of belt they were talking about just didn't fit. "Thanks, Al." Johnny started out of the shop and then stopped and walked back. "What other kinds of belts are valuable?"

"Concho belts." Al indicated one on display in the window, others hanging behind the counter.

Even farther out. Johnny shook his head.

"Well, hell," Al said, "they still make money belts. If you're looking for one, they have them in Bean's catalogue."

Johnny smiled suddenly, showing the white teeth. *"Qué cosa!"* He nodded. "Thanks, Al." He walked back to headquarters to perch on Tony Lopez's desk— Sergeant Tony Lopez.

"What we have," Johnny said, and explained. "Probably in the snow since that big January storm." He raised his hand, fingers spread, and ticked off points: "Belt missing. Money belt? Could make sense. Pants too big. Why? No missing bulletin on him. Why? He looks like a *turista*. Where would he have been staying? How did he get up there in the middle of the ski slope without being seen? And why?"

"*Basta*," Tony said. "Enough. I don't know the answers."

"Then," Johnny said, "start finding out." He slid off the desk. "I've got a hunch."

Tony looked unhappy. When this Indian began plucking ideas out of the air, there was no telling where the end might lie—

The telephone on Tony's desk rang. He picked it up, spoke his name, listened, handed the phone to Johnny. It was Doc Easy at the hospital, and Doc's voice was hard. "I haven't even got to your man yet, son," he said. "I've been busy." He paused. "Another Spanish boy. Overdose of bad heroin."

Nothing changed in Johnny's face. "Dead?"

"Dead."

"I'll come over," Johnny said, and hung up. He looked down at Tony. "Number three," he said. He paused. "And we haven't any idea where the stuff's coming from."

2

In man's memory there had always been drugs in Santo Cristo. Perhaps, as some said, it was the proximity to Mexico that was the cause. That border stretching from San Ysidro to Brownsville, across California, Arizona, New Mexico, and Texas, was a sieve through which narcotics, and people, could flow almost at will. Oh, frequently, usually on *information received,* the Border Patrol made a hit. But how much drugs and how many people they missed was anybody's guess. So many men could only be in so many places at one time.

"But this is different," Doc Easy said. "This stuff kills. Any poor fool who mainlines a shot of this horse is a deado." Doc was usually mild. He was angry now.

"You said overdose," Johnny said.

"Any dose is an overdose."

The victim was a Spanish-American boy with a driver's license that showed him to be just twenty-two. His name was Ruben Martinez. "I know something about him," Johnny said, "now what is it?" He stared thoughtfully at the still clothed body. Then, "Of course.

Those combat boots." He looked at Doc. "There was a picture of him in the paper." His face and his voice were expressionless. "He was standing in the Oval Room of the White House getting the Medal of Honor."

"So," Doc said, "he lived through Viet Nam and came home to die. That's a fine commentary on something." He turned away. "I'll get to your other one."

Mrs. Martinez was not quite forty, looked over sixty, and was at the moment incoherent, sobbing. There was a girl of about sixteen with her now, holding a baby. There was also a priest.

"Information, padre," Johnny said. He spoke in Spanish. "You knew the boy?"

"I have known all the children. There are fifteen. Luisa," he gestured at the baby, "is the newest. Ruben was the first."

They had moved across the small room. Johnny spoke quietly. "Do you know how he died?"

"I have heard—rumor, no more than that."

"He was a heroin addict, padre. He died of a bad dose of the drug."

The priest was silent.

"Your parish," Johnny said. "Do you know who supplies the drugs?"

"Others have asked," the priest said. He shook his head.

Across the room the sobbing rose in volume. The girl holding her baby sister made soothing noises. The baby began to cry.

"This is the third death, padre," Johnny said. "That makes it neither more nor less important than the others, but it does tell us that there may be more unless we can find the man who is selling the bad heroin." He paused. "Did you know that Ruben was an addict?"

"I had heard."

"Are any of his brothers? Sisters?"

"I think not," the priest said. "Ruben acquired the habit in Viet Nam. I have heard that many do. His brothers, sisters—" He shook his head. "For the older ones alcohol, perhaps. Marijuana occasionally, maybe. But heroin, no. Heroin is too expensive."

"You know that, padre?"

"I have heard." Back to square one.

Johnny walked out to his pick-up. A group of four boys, teenagers, watched him, their faces carefully expressionless. No point in trying to talk with them, Johnny thought, got into the pick-up, and drove away. In the mirror he saw the boys watching after him. *I am the enemy;* the words came unbidden into his mind. A year ago, he thought, the concept would not have bothered him; now it was vaguely painful. Because of Cassie, of course, who had taught him to care.

Cassie—Cassandra Enright, Ph.D., anthropologist— was at her desk in the small office of the museum. She was a tall, slim, rounded girl, café au lait in color; dressed in her working clothes of flannel shirt, wheat Levis, and boots. On a rug at her feet a half-grown collie-shepherd-husky mix watched her adoringly and from time to time thumped the floor with his tail. Cassie had a visitor.

His name was Paul Harper, and he was relatively

new in town, apparently well-heeled, pleasant, friendly, a good skier. He spoke with a faint New England accent. "You might look at it this way, doctor," he said. "Twenty-five sections, sixteen thousand acres of nothing but piñon, juniper, cholla, and grama grass." He had learned his vegetation well. "It is not really good cattle land, and it is useless for agriculture."

Cassie could not argue the points; they were axiomatic.

"And in other parts of the country," Harper said, "people are crowded together like sardines in a can, no room to stretch, or even to breathe. Think what a piece of land, one acre, two, five acres would mean to them."

On the floor, Chico thumped his tail for attention. Cassie reached down to pull his ear gently while she did mental arithmetic. "Four—five thousand houses," she said. "Twenty thousand people. Your problem is water, Mr. Harper. Where can you get water for all those people?"

Harper smiled. "Deep wells. The water is there. It's just a question of drilling for it."

It was thirsty land, this high mesa country, and water was, and had always been, its key. Cassie shook her head. "I'm not a geologist," she said, "or a hydrologist, but I question whether there is that much water—" She paused. "Without lowering the water table," she said.

Harper smiled and shrugged. "I've heard that. An old rancher made a point of telling me. He said that if his wells went dry, and he couldn't fill his stock tanks—"

The smile spread. "He sounded like something out of *Bonanza*."

Cassie was unsmiling. "He is, Mr. Harper," she said. "His name is Ben Hart, and if he thought you were stealing his water—" She shook her head slowly. "I can't help you," she said. "Ecology is a big word these days, and I suppose by some stretch of the imagination an anthropologist's support would carry some weight, but I can't see it. I'm sorry."

Suddenly the little office was still. On the floor, Chico's head came up and his black nose began to work, probing for understanding. The silence grew, stretched. "I wish you would change your mind, doctor," Harper said at last. He stood up, smiling no longer. "I really do," he added, and walked out.

Tony Lopez said, "On the ski slope body, no bulletins, no missing persons queries that fit. If he carried a wallet, and who doesn't, it's gone too. We don't know—" He stopped. Young Pete Tomlin stood in the doorway with a cloth-wrapped bundle in his hands.

"Come in," Johnny said. "What have you got?"

The boy carried the bundle as if it were fragile. He laid it on Tony's desk. "I hope I did right," he said. "I mean, you know, I got to thinking, so I went back to where I found him and poked around with my poles. I found this." He opened the bundle. It contained a stubby handgun in a clip holster. The metal of the gun showed rust.

Tony stared at the holster, frowning. He looked at Johnny. "Left-handed? The clip is on the wrong side otherwise."

Johnny shook his head slowly. "It's a hideaway holster, fits inside your waistband, only the clip shows outside." So now, he thought, they knew why the man's pants were loose around the middle. Now, too, they could guess that the man habitually wore a handgun, which put an entirely different light on the matter. To Pete, "You did fine," Johnny said. "Thanks." And when the boy was gone, "Send the gun over to Saul Pentland at the lab," he said to Tony, "and see what he can tell us about it."

Tony said, "Check the serial number?"

Johnny nodded without enthusiasm. "Of course. But you won't find any registration." The man who had ended under the snow being skied over all winter, he thought, was beginning to look very much like a pro who would not carry a registered handgun. And what in the world was a pro doing here in Santo Cristo? Answer me that, Juan Felipe.

He put the same question to Cassie that night after dinner in Cassie's house, sitting companionably close on the sofa facing the piñon fire, Chico dozing at Cassie's feet. "We don't have," Johnny said, "at least I don't think we have the kind of organized crime that runs to big-city clothes and hideaway holsters. So what was he doing here?" His smile was fond. "Ideas, chica?"

It was always flattering to be asked, because, Cassie thought, he meant the questions seriously. She said slowly, "You're sure he was just a visitor?"

"We're not sure of anything, but it makes more sense that he was just passing through. If he'd been staying here for any length of time, somebody would probably have missed him, no?''

''Not,'' Cassie said, ''if it was the somebody who put him in the snow.'' She shivered faintly.

Johnny thought about it. He nodded. ''A point, chica, but I'm still betting he was traveling.''

Chico stirred and thumped the floor with his tail. Johnny reached down to seize the dog's muzzle and shake it gently.

''Traveling salesman,'' Cassie said. She was smiling. ''Carrying a gun to persuade customers to buy his wares.'' She meant it facetiously, but again Johnny was silent, thoughtful.

He said at last, ''It could be.'' He smiled suddenly and the white teeth flashed. ''There is that kind of salesman. He sells protection.'' He shook his head then, and the smile was gone. ''I think we would have heard something.''

Cassie said, ''A courier?''

''Spell that one out, chica.''

''A messenger? I'm thinking wild, Johnny.''

''Keep at it.'' He smiled again. ''Beautiful *and* bright, *fantástico!* Keep going.''

Cassie said slowly, ''Do they always look the part? The higher-ups in organized crime, I mean? Do they always look like Edward G. Robinson?'' She paused. Johnny watched her quietly with that bone-bred patience of his. ''What I mean,'' Cassie said, ''is do some of them look just like ordinary successful businessmen? Do they have wives and children? Do they take vacations, maybe winter vacations? Do they stay at luxury hotels like the Lodge? Do they ski?'' She was silent.

"Don't stop now," Johnny said.

"I'm just guessing, Johnny."

He nodded in silence, waiting.

"Maybe," Cassie said, "the dead man was bringing a message of some kind to somebody here on vacation. Maybe—"

"The belt," Johnny said. "Suppose Al Packer was right, a money belt. It would fit with the hideaway holster." He paused. "Suppose, chica, he wasn't a salesman, or a messenger. Suppose he was a collector. Suppose his job was traveling around picking up payments or making deliveries—"

"For what?" Cassie said. "Deliveries of what?"

"It could be several things. Stock theft is a big thing, for one. You steal, say, one hundred shares of IBM from a brokerage house. The shares will be missed, and their serial numbers known, so you take those shares to someone at another brokerage house maybe in another city, and he steals another hundred shares of IBM and replaces them with those you have. The stock inventory at his brokerage house checks out, so nobody bothers to look at the serial numbers until the stock is sold, transferred." Johnny spread his hands. "Then with the hundred shares whose serial numbers are not listed as stolen, you get a bank loan up to, say, eighty per cent of the face value of the stock, and there you have cash in hand." He paused. "That's one thing."

"What are others?"

It was still in his mind, of course. He was thinking of Mrs. Martinez and her fifteen children, Ruben, the oldest, now dead in the hospital. "Drugs," he said. "Delivery of the drugs and collection of the payment for them could be separate operations. That would account for a money belt and a handgun to protect it." He smiled suddenly. "All guesswork, of course, chica. Tomorrow we'll start looking into it." He paused, smiling still. "Right now," he said.

"Yes?"

"Guapa," Johnny said, *"guapíssima,* a very sexy female, chica, and right now I'd much rather be doing other things than guessing about a dead man."

Cassie's smile was serene. "Why don't you show me what you have in mind?"

3

The unidentified dead man from the ski slope made the local paper, of course, front page; whereas buried deep inside the paper next to the crossword puzzle was the mere announcement that a Mass would be said for the soul of Ruben Martinez, beloved son of Carlos and Juanita Martinez of 521 Camino Real.

"No record on the man," Tony Lopez said, "or on the handgun." He was watching Johnny's face. "More visions?" he said.

"He was here sometime in January for a guess," Johnny said. "If he came by car, where is the car? If he flew in, how did he get to town from the airport? Taxi? Where did he stay, and is his luggage still there? Because he didn't have it with him in the snow."

Tony sighed and nodded. "I know. Think."

Doc Easy said, "Somebody used a knife on him, somebody who knew what he was doing." He touched the back of his neck. "Just below the occipital bulge into the spinal cord." He snapped his fingers. "It's called pithing. Quick, and no muss. Then he lay on his side for a time—''

"He was on his back in the snow," Johnny said.

"I can't help that, son. He lay on his side for some time after death. Dependent lividity; and the tissue doesn't lie."

Johnny thought about it. "That knife," he said. "Small blade?"

Doc nodded.

"How about an ice pick? That used to be popular."

"Before your time, son."

"I've heard about it," Johnny said. "Murder, Incorporated. The ice pick was their specialty." He shook his head liking the implications less and less, because the killing sounded professional and the dead man looked to be a professional, and that meant—Johnny didn't know what that meant, but it wasn't the sudden-crime-of-anger Santo Cristo normally had.

Saul Pentland at the police lab said, "Clothing tailor-made, no labels except in the raincoat—Alligator, sold everywhere. Wristwatch," Saul smiled and shook his head, "still running, right on time. One of those electric watches that runs on a battery. You replace the battery once a year." Saul was a big man, an ex–offensive tackle for the Dallas Cowboys. In his white coat he looked big as a bear. "Where's his belt?"

"We'd like to know."

"I can't help you much," Saul said. "His shoes—" He shrugged. "Good quality Florsheim, size 9B." He shrugged again. "After three months in the snow, the soles don't tell much."

"The handgun," Johnny said.

"Thirty-eight caliber, five-shot double-action revolver with a two-inch barrel." Saul paused. "It's called Undercover, and at sixteen ounces it's about the smallest thirty-eight made in this country. A lot of cops carry them off-duty." He paused again. "All five rounds are live. He hadn't fired the gun."

Thinking of the ice pick or knife, "He didn't have the chance," Johnny said.

The city of Santo Cristo lay in the foothills at an altitude of 7,000 feet. At this height juniper and piñon grew in near-symbiosis in company with chamisa, cactus, Apache plume, and the ubiquitous grama grass. Where there was water, there were cottonwoods.

The high dry air was tonic, and in other years the tuberculosis sanitarium had drawn patients from as far as the eastern seaboard; just as in summer the Lodge had drawn visitors for the climate and the peace. Now the sanitarium was a monastery, and the Lodge drew as many customers in winter for the skiing as in summer for horseback riding and tennis and swimming.

It was to the Lodge that afternoon that Tony Lopez went as a matter of continuing routine, carrying with him a picture of the dead man which made him look very dead indeed. Sam Christopher, resident Lodge manager, studied the picture without enthusiasm.

"Dressed like that?" Sam said. "Up in the snow? It doesn't make sense."

Tony agreed that it made no sense. "Do you recognize him?"

Sam shook his head. "Not one of our guests." He

paused. Truculence appeared. "Somebody say he was?"

Tony sighed. There was, he had long ago decided, nothing more touchy than a touchy Anglo. He stood six inches taller than Sam Christopher, and he supposed that had something to do with it, too. "Nobody," he said, "is pointing a finger at your hotel, Mr. Christopher. I'm checking every place he might have stayed, and obviously your place is on the list."

"We don't have guests who go out and get themselves dead on ski slopes. We're a family hotel."

Through the arched black iron grill, Tony could see waiters quietly setting up the dining tables. "Maybe he came here to eat," he said. It was a sudden hunch, and he pinned no great hopes on it.

"He did not," Sam Christopher said.

Tony resented both the tone and the attitude. "How can you be sure?" he said, and he allowed a little edge to creep into his voice. "Do you vet every guest who comes here to eat? To have a drink?" He paused. "Are you here all day every day?"

Sam Christopher took a deep breath. He swelled. "Look—"

"No," Tony said, "you look. This is a murder case, and we'll just see if any of your waiters remember our man." He went to the grill, opened it, and walked inside. Sam Christopher trotted at his heels.

It was a long shot, of course, but, as Tony told Johnny later, "It figured that he had to eat somewhere, and the Lodge has maybe the best food in town. One of the waiters remembered him. You know why?" Tony wrin-

kled his nose in distaste. "Because of the drink he or-
dered. Dubonnet and tonic—did you ever hear of it?"

Johnny had not; he doubted if many people had. He
said, "But he wasn't staying at the Lodge?"

Tony shook his head. "Just there for one meal—
dinner."

"Alone?"

"He was the guest of Mr. and Mrs. Sonny March.
They were staying at the Lodge like they do every win-
ter. They left two weeks ago." Tony shrugged.
"They're somewhere in the Caribbean now."

The chinook wind had stopped blowing, but the
damage was done: ski season was over. No one knew
exactly how or why the change took place, but it happened every year: the lifts and the slopes were suddenly
empty, and the tennis courts in town were suddenly
filled.

Oh, a handful of diehards refused to acknowledge
the change of season and labored up into the high country where, above the 11,000-foot timber-line, the snow
was still deep enough for sport; but the prevailing attitude of Santo Cristo had already altered subtly from
winter-orientation to anticipation of summer.

"Picnics, chica," Johnny told Cassie, and Chico at
their feet thumped the floor with his tail.

The mood was general. Old Ben Hart on the telephone to Congressman Mark Hawley said, "How long
has it been since anybody threw a real honest-to-God
barbecue?"

Mark Hawley thought about it. "I'm damned if I can
remember." Both men were well into their seventies,

and on a fine late-spring-early-summer day nostalgia ran strong. "It's an idea. There's that outfit down in Texas that puts them on."

Ben Hart snorted. "Is that what we've come to, for God's sake? Can't even whomp up our own cookout? Why, hells bells, I'll have a couple of oil drums cut in half, fill them with charcoal, slaughter a couple of steers, churn up some hot sauce, and away we go. How about that?"

The congressman was smiling now. Once upon a time, and not so long ago at that, this wide, sometimes wild, world had been young, and he and Ben right in the middle of it not infrequently stirring up dust. Memory was pleasant. "I'll have the sauce churned up. How many gallons you need?" He paused. "How many people? Two, three hundred?"

Ben was silent, thoughtful. "That ought to do it."

"Tortillas," the congressman said, "and beans, beer, coffee, four, five cases of whiskey—" Enthusiasm was mounting. "Hoo, boy! Why didn't you think of this before?"

"Because," Ben said, "we've turned so goddamned civilized." Pause. "Maybe some venison too, and I suppose *cabrito.*"

"Apple pies," the congressman said, and he added, "Deer is out of season." Silence was eloquent. "Oh, well," the congressman said, "you can always claim self-defense."

Ben owned sixty sections of land, some forty thousand acres of mesa, piñon, juniper, cholla, grama grass, and some water, enough. He leased another ten thousand acres. His ranch house, eight miles in from the cattle guard at the highway, was of adobe, two stories of three-foot-thick walls and enormous windows facing the distant mountains. Ben himself was a great bear of a man, customarily dressed in jeans and boots and a flannel shirt—cotton in summer, wool in winter—the sleeves rolled partway up his massive forearms. When, infrequently, he drove into town it was at the wheel of a monster Cadillac known to every policeman in the county.

He drove in on this bright day, found a parking space large enough for the Cadillac, and strolled around to see Cassie at the museum. Cassie was one of his favorites; he admired her female presence, and he enjoyed her intelligent erudition. He sat in her small office and pulled Chico's ears gently while he talked. "Fellow named Harper," he said, "a dude. You've seen him?"

Cassie spoke of Harper's visit.

"There's money behind him," Ben said, "that's plain. And we aren't going to keep this country the way it is forever. That's plain too."

Cassie smiled. She was fond of the old man who was, really, an anachronism, a complete throwback to the Anglos who came and took and held against all comers what land they thought they needed, or wanted. And that concept brought history to mind. "First," she said, "as far as we know, the Indians who lived in ruins we're just now uncovering—in the Grand Canyon, and over on the edge of Arroyo Hondo. Then the visible remains of the cliff-dwellers—Bandelier, Mesa Verde. Next the Pueblo Indians and the Navajo-Apache invasion. Then the Spanish, Mexican rule, even for a time Texas." She paused. "Then the first wave of Anglos.

Now the groundswell of more Anglos from the East."
She smiled again, sadly this time. "Progress, Ben."

"Time was," Ben said, "when a dude like Harper
coming out here, he behaved himself or he was shown
the light and sent back where he came from, sometimes
in a box. I guess things are different now." He waved
one great hand in a gesture of dismissal. "What I came
for, honey, aside from the pleasure of just looking at
you—I'm going to whomp me up a barbecue and I'll
want you and Johnny on hand, hear?" He heaved himself out of his chair and stood for a moment looking
down at the girl, obviously with something on his mind.
But in the end all he said was, "Be seeing you, honey."

Cassie watched his broad back swinging down the
hall and wondered what it was he had left unsaid.

Ben strolled out into the plaza. There were *turistas;*
there were always *turistas.* Ben didn't mind; in a way
he was proud that they would want to come and see his
country, his town—long as they behaved themselves.
And some *turistas,* not many, but some, were cute little
heifers with their tight bottoms and bouncing breasts,
a pleasure for an old man to study on. As he walked
toward the Federal Building and Mark Hawley's office,
his eyes, perpetually squinting beneath the battered hat
brim, watched the passing parade.

Mark Hawley was in. He got up and poured two
shots of that fine bourbon of his, handed one to Ben,
and closed the door before he sat down at his desk
again. "Been thinking," he said. "You planning this
hoedown out of sheer friendliness and the goodness of
your heart?"

Even back when he and Hawley had carried on their

historic feud, Ben thought, he had always been willing to grant that the congressman was smart; Mark Hawley had never been known to confuse his ass with a hole in the ground. "Not entirely," Ben said. He sipped the whiskey. Far better than fine wine.

"Thought so," Hawley said. "You're a crafty son of a bitch. What're you up to?"

Ben told him, and Hawley listened quietly. When Ben was done, "Between us," Hawley said, "I agree. I don't think there's enough water for all the people Harper's talking about, but even if we had the water, I'd sure as hell rather not see this country looking like Arlington, Virginia." He had a sip of his own whiskey, finished it, got up, and went to the cupboard for the bottle. He came back to his desk. "On the other hand," he said, "I can't very sensibly come out foursquare against progress, either."

Ben nodded. "I kind of figured you'd say that."

"Goddam it," Hawley said, "what else—"

"Now don't get your ass in an uproar." Ben's voice was easy, amused. "All I want from you is a list of people, state legislators, official-types, men with influence, that kind of thing." He poured himself another drink.

"And," Hawley said, "you feed them barbecued beef and beans and bourbon to soften them up." He nodded.

"Anything wrong with that?" Ben's voice was still amused. "Seems to me that's about how you got elected in the first place, ridin' from hoedown to hoedown, kissin' the babies, oglin' the women and drinkin' with the menfolk."

True enough. "Nothing at all wrong with it," Hawley said. The hell of it was that nowadays you got on television, talking to a goddam tube instead of to live people. He sighed. "I'll have Bessie draw you up a list. You'll know every one of them, but maybe we can help a bit by cutting out the culls." He was silent for a few moments. "You're going about it the right way," he said, "fighting Harper and his big ideas through channels." He paused, whiskey glass in hand. "But what happens if you can't whip him, if all the planning commissions and the legislature can see is land values going up, business boom, people crowding in here to spend more money—and never mind what happens to the country, to the water table?" He thought he knew the answer.

"If he drills deep wells," Ben said, "and my wells go dry and I can't keep my stock tanks full—" He shook his head slowly. "The Harper dude and I will go round and round and one of us is going to get skinned up."

Hawley believed him. He also approved. "Pour yourself another drink," he said. He studied Ben's face. "Something else on your mind?"

"Cassie." Ben paused. "And Johnny—"

"What about them?"

"Why don't they get married?"

"Why don't you ask them?"

Ben nodded. "I was tempted to. Just now when I saw Cassie. But I didn't."

"Because you'd be sticking your finger in her eye." There was approval in the congressman's voice. "They'll work it out their own way. Maybe they'll marry, maybe they won't." He leaned back in his chair. "You know what she told me once? I've never forgotten it. She said she was a black chick with a go-go dancer's carcass and a head stuffed to the eyeballs with anthropological erudition and where in the world was she going to find a man who'd take all of that seriously."

Ben sighed, nodded, and reached for the bottle. "And Johnny carries a chip on his shoulder too, and I can't blame him." He paused, glass in hand. "We're a bunch of sons of bitches, all of us Anglos, you know that?"

"I've never denied it," the congressman said.

4

The sign that hung above the intersection of alley and street read: BITS AND PIECES. In small neat letters in the corner of the sign: By Appointment. There might have been added, but had not been: Newton Berry, Prop. The first thing you noticed as you entered the shop was the smell of incense. On this morning another smell had been added: the acrid odor of an explosion.

The windows were blown out, and inside the shop there was broken, jumbled confusion of the stock, invariably one-of-a-kind, which ranged from quality Southwestern Indian baskets and pottery to a large totem pole from Alaska to ceremonial masks from Africa, Burmese amber, Chinese jade, Coptic art from Ethiopia, French kitchen pieces of heavy copper and true antiquity, German beer steins, Guatemalan cottons, soapstone carvings from Baffin Bay—in short, bits and pieces, or, in Spanish, *cosas,* things.

Berry, summoned from home by a police telephone call, stared at the mess and almost wept. He was in his fifties, slim and active, customarily dressed, as now, in neatly pressed hand-tailored lightweight gabardine trousers, a sport shirt, and desert boots. His hands were shaking as he got out a cigarette, fitted it into an ivory holder, and managed to light it. "I don't understand!" It was almost a wail. "I simply don't understand!"

Jim Ball, electrician, assistant chief of the volunteer fire department, picked his way out through the wreckage. "The center of the explosion was over there," he said, pointing back into the shop.

"But how?" Berry said. "How could they get in?" And then the recurrent theme: "Why? I simply don't understand!"

"The how is simple enough," Ball said. "They dropped the explosive down the chimney." He eyed Berry shrewdly. "The why somebody else'll have to answer." He looked at his watch. "Time to go to work," he said, and walked out to his truck.

Tony Lopez perched on Johnny's desk. "It's a mess," Tony said. "Berry's going to break down and cry any minute, and I don't suppose you can blame him, all that stuff he loves." He paused. "You think kids?"

"No," Johnny said. He was not usually positive, but this time conviction was strong.

"Berry says he hasn't any idea why," Tony said.

"Then he'd damn well better find out." Johnny paused. "And I think he will. A phone call?" He shook his head. "They can't count on the phone still working. Probably it isn't."

Tony opened his mouth and then shut it again in silence. There were times when he thought of this Johnny

Ortiz as some kind of *brujo,* a witch, conjuring up images other men did not see. He waited.

"Does he have a Post Office box?" Johnny said suddenly.

"There are many things I do not know, amigo," Tony said patiently in Spanish. "That is one of them."

"Then go find out." The trick, of course, was to put yourself, if you could, in the mind of the person who had committed the criminal act. Johnny decided that it was time he started thinking along professional lines. "And if he does have a box," he said, "get a look at the mail that's in it today. The answer ought to be there."

It was. The address on the envelope and the writing inside were characterless block letters, so symmetrical that they had to have been drawn through a lettering guide. The message was brief: THIS IS JUST A WARNING.

Berry, in Johnny's office, shook his head in disbelief. "I simply don't understand," he said. "A warning about what?" His hands still shook and he had trouble lighting a fresh cigarette. Through smoke he watched Johnny's face, and, being a sensitive and imaginative man, found the harsh Indian lines and the angry eyes far from reassuring.

"Somebody," Johnny said, "doesn't like something you're doing. That's the obvious inference, no? Now what would that something be?"

"My poor *cosas,*" Berry said. "How could they offend anyone?"

"I don't think it's your poor *cosas.*"

"Then?" Berry spread his hands. He was a very

civilized person, and even now he could manage the light touch. "I'm sure no one fancies that I have been carrying on with his wife, lieutenant."

Silently Johnny agreed. Nor could he quite see Berry in any other role that was enough of a threat to bring about this kind of professional retaliation. But there it was. "You'd better think about it," he said. "Because if you can't figure out what you're doing that somebody doesn't like, you'll probably keep right on doing it, and the next time it may not be your *cosas* that take the beating."

Berry closed his eyes and shivered. "I can't stand even the thought of physical violence, lieutenant."

"Then you'd better start thinking," Johnny said. "Hard."

And when Berry had gone back to his shop to try to bring order out of chaos, Tony perched again on the corner of Johnny's desk. "Does it make sense?" Tony said.

Johnny thought that it did, unpleasant sense. "A professional job," he said. "They had no doubts. They were confident enough to put the warning note in the mail yesterday instead of waiting to see if the bomb actually did go off."

Tony thought about it. He nodded. The goddam trouble was that it was so clear when it was explained to you, which made the fact that you hadn't seen it yourself all the more demeaning. And there was probably more that he couldn't see either. "Go on," he said.

"Pros," Johnny said, "don't use muscle just for the fun of it."

True enough, even axiomatic. "Maybe they made a mistake," Tony said.

"How can you mistake Berry?" Johnny said. "Or his shop? His *cosas?* He's one of a kind, even here in Santo Cristo."

"Okay," Tony said. "Then you tell me. How does it make sense?"

The conclusion was inescapable. "Berry's lying. He knows perfectly well what he's doing that somebody doesn't like, and he's wetting his pants about it." Johnny paused. "And I can't really blame him."

Tony Lopez was a thorough man, not easily turned aside. He covered the highway motel area, the three hotels, and two of the four motels in town before he struck paydirt. At the Mid-Towner Motor Hotel, single rate: $14–$18, the desk clerk said yes, he recognized the picture of the dead man, but the manager said no, and the desk clerk promptly changed his mind.

Tony sighed. "All right," he said, "let's go. Both of you."

The manager's name was Bert Walker, a stylish dresser who strutted when he walked, his toes turned well out. "I'm busy, sergeant," he said, and smiled the smile he reserved for unknown and unimportant guests without reservations.

"Suit yourself," Tony said. "You can come along quietly, or I'll put handcuffs on you and drag you." He still held the picture in his hand and he shook it gently at the desk clerk while his eyes did not leave Bert Walker's face.

Walker said, "Now wait a minute, sergeant. The

mayor is a very good friend of mine—" He stopped. He swallowed. "Let's go into my office," he said. "I'm sure we can straighten out this—misunderstanding." The smile was gone.

"You, too," Tony said to the desk clerk.

Walker opened his mouth and then shut it again in silence.

"I don't get it," Tony said later to Johnny. "The desk clerk changed his mind again and even came up with a name: Walter Wilson, from New York City. And then Walker suddenly remembered and said yes, Mr. Wilson had stayed with them, but when the girl in the accounting office tried to find the card for Walter Wilson, it wasn't there." Tony was silent, puzzled.

Johnny thought about it. He said at last, "What about his luggage?"

Tony spread his hands. His shrug was eloquent. "Wilson could have checked out and taken it with him. There's no record."

Johnny shook his head. "It would have turned up somewhere, airline, bus terminal—" Again the head-shake, in annoyance this time. "Walter Wilson, New York City," he said. "That doesn't tell us a thing."

"He drank Dubonnet and tonic," Tony said. And then, watching the change on Johnny's face, *"Dios!* Have I done it again?"

"The bartender at the Mid-Towner," Johnny said. "He might remember something." He paused. "Try all the bars in town if you have to."

"I've done it again," said Tony.

* * *

It was Cassie's idea that finally provided the major clue concerning Walter Wilson from New York City. "Every now and again," Cassie told Johnny, "old photos turn up at the museum, and sometimes we can identify the buildings and the people, and sometimes we can't. Then if it seems important, two or three unidentified strangers around a known Territorial Governor, for example, we ask the paper to run the photo to see if any readers can help us."

"Perfectly simple," Johnny said, shaking his head in wonder. "The only thing is, why didn't I think of it?" Tony Lopez would have recognized the feeling.

"Sometimes," Cassie said, "you're surprised by what you find out."

It was a surprise, in the large form of Mary Margaret McDade, Miss McDade, proprietress of the what-not shop in the Sol y Lomas shopping center. She swept into Johnny's office, shaking the afternoon paper as if it were a club. "You want to know about this man? Well, I can certainly tell you." She perched her broad beam on the visitor's chair. "I don't wonder. I certainly don't wonder that something happened to him. He deserved it. He certainly did. And the wonder is that more hasn't happened because of that—place!" She paused for breath.

Johnny asked which place.

"That—that—they call it an art theatre. Art indeed! Films of naked females, and naked males, too, doing things that—that defy mention!"

Johnny wondered how Miss McDade had obtained her knowledge of what was shown on the mini-screen of the local skin-flick house. He thought it better not to ask. "About this man," he said. "What was his connection with the theatre?"

"He went there. I saw him. Not once; four or five times, right in the middle of the afternoon, bold as brass. One day he was there twice, as if he couldn't see enough of—of what they show on that screen!" Miss McDade breathed hard.

Johnny thought about it. He said at last, "Did you know the man?"

"Certainly not!" There was a brief pause. "Although you would be surprised, you would indeed, if I told you the names of men, prominent men, I've watched going in there. If their wives knew!" Miss McDade shook her head as she reflected on male perfidy.

Gently, Johnny told himself, lest sudden resentment slow the torrent of righteous anger. "How did you happen to notice him, Miss McDade?" Although, he told himself later, he ought to have known the answer.

The fact was that Miss McDade's major occupation, interrupted only by the demands of an occasional customer, was keeping her eye on the skin-flick house and everyone who entered it. "Oh," she said, "not the Spanish or the poor working Anglos, although, the good Lord knows, they ought to have better places to spend their money, and I don't mean in saloons, either!" She drew her breath on the dead run, Johnny thought; her pauses were almost imperceptible. "But the decently dressed men who have no business, absolutely no business patronizing that kind of filth, I notice them and mark them down for what they are, lecherous beasts. And this one looked like a decent, God-fearing, respectable man, but I ask you, what was he doing going into that—place time after time after time?''

''I don't know, Miss McDade,'' Johnny said, ''but I'm going to try to find out.'' He could not resist adding, straight-faced, ''So if you see me going into the theatre, it will be in the line of duty.''

''I should hope so. I should certainly hope so!'' Miss McDade heaved herself off the chair.

Johnny rose with her. ''I thank you for coming forward,'' he said.

''My duty; my plain, clear duty as a decent citizen.'' Miss McDade set off down the corridor reminding Johnny of a large ship under full sail.

Johnny walked into Tony's office and perched on his desk. ''The dirty movie house,'' he said. ''What do we know about it?''

Tony smirked. ''They show films of pretty girls, amigo, wearing no clothes and doing things my mother would not approve of.'' He paused for reflection. ''On the other hand,'' he said, ''the fact that I am here indicates that my mother is not totally ignorant of such things, no?''

''Neither,'' Johnny said, ''is Miss Mary Margaret McDade.'' He explained.

Tony sighed. His opinion of humanity was not high. ''Some get their jollies one way, some another. Me,'' he paused, ''I prefer the real thing. Pictures don't really turn me on.''

It was the obvious inference, Johnny thought, but he did not like it. The handgun in the hideaway holster, the missing belt which might very well have been a money belt—''I won't buy it,'' he said. ''If Wilson was a pro, and that's the way it looks, then he'd have kept his mind on his business and not spent his time watching porno films. He—'' He stopped. His eyebrows rose.

Tony said gently, "Tell me, amigo. Another vision?''

"Suppose," Johnny said slowly, carefully, "you wanted to meet somebody you didn't particularly want to be seen with? Where would you do it?''

Tony waved one hand. "Dark street, country road, parked car—'' He stopped. "At night,'' he said. He nodded. "But in a dirty movie house where it's dark, and nobody pays any attention to anybody else because everybody's a little embarrassed about being there—'' He nodded once more. The Indian *brujo*, he thought, had done it again. "That would account for his going in twice in one afternoon, no?''

"It would,'' Johnny said. He was silent for a few moments. "It might account for something else, too.'' He was reaching far out, he told himself, but in a vague, gruesome way, it did make sense. "The way he was killed. Knife, maybe ice pick into the spinal cord.'' He looked down at Tony. "Do you see it? You've got to go in-between the vertebrae. It isn't easy. You hit bone, you've missed your chance. It isn't like a knife under the ribs or across the throat.''

Tony, listening, understanding, said softly, *"Madre de Dios!"*

"Yes,'' Johnny said. "You want your man to be perfectly still.'' He paused. "Like, maybe, sitting watching, or pretending to watch, a movie screen.'' He paused again. "And you know he's going to be there, because he and you arranged a meeting.'' He slid down from the desk. "Let's go visit the dirty movie house.''

5

Paul Harper drove out to the Lodge at less than his normal speed. He was not a timorous man, but when, as now, he was summoned to the Presence, he tended to assess his position very carefully indeed; and as he considered it now, he was not at all convinced that it was secure; his foot was reluctant on the accelerator.

It was Sam Christopher himself at the reception desk, and there was no need for Sam to check his room listings; he carried information on important guests in his head. "Mr. Ross and his party are in Cottage A," he told Harper. "The house telephone is over there."

Harper placed his call on the house phone, listened, hung up, sighed, and began the slow walk out to Cottage A. The day was bright, the sun warm, and the sky overhead an unbelievable blue. Harper was aware only of the crunching of gravel beneath his feet. It sounded, he thought, like breaking bones.

As he walked up to the *portal* of Cottage A, the door burst open and a teenage girl, all tanned slim legs and arms in a brief tennis dress, flew past him waving a metal racquet and laughing. "Hi!" she said, and was gone immediately down the gravel path. And there in the doorway was Ross himself.

He was not a big man, but in his quiet voice and controlled gestures, his easy smile that never seemed to reach his eyes, you saw something of his force. "Pauley," he said. "Come in." He held the door wide. "Long time."

"Last December, Mr. Ross." On a cold gray day in Westchester, six inches of snow covering the rolling lawns visible from the library windows.

Ross did not close the door. To the woman sitting in the room he said, "This is Paul Harper, dear. He and I are going to talk a little business. Why don't you go watch Cindy's tennis lesson?"

The woman rose, smiling. "Always business," she said to Harper.

"I'm sorry," Harper said, which was neither more nor less than truth. He watched the woman walk out. The door closed.

Ross walked to a carved wood cabinet. Over his shoulder he said, "Drink, Pauley? Bourbon, if I remember."

"Yes, Mr. Ross."

"Sit down, Pauley."

Harper sat down. He accepted his drink and held it carefully, untasted. Ross sat down in a facing chair. "So now," he said, "we know what happened to Walter Wilson."

"Yes, Mr. Ross."

"What else do we know?" Ross's eyes were brown,

shiny, and steady on Harper's face; they were uncomfortingly expressionless.

"He just—dropped out of sight," Harper said. "One day he was here and everything was fine. The next day he was gone. No trace at the motel, nothing. It was snowing hard and things in town were pretty confused, traffic tied up, that kind of thing. But I tried to find him—" Harper lifted his free hand in a gesture of helplessness. "He just wasn't around."

"So your letter said." Ross's voice held no trace of emotion. "He was gone. The money was gone. Even his luggage was gone."

"Yes, Mr. Ross."

"You thought maybe he had skipped."

"Yes, Mr. Ross."

"But," Ross said, "he hadn't." He waited, but there was no comment. "Drink your drink, Pauley."

Harper drank. It was fine smooth bourbon, but it tasted bitter. He set the glass down carefully.

"What ideas do you have?" Ross said in that quiet, uninflected voice. "Who did it? How? Why? Where? How did Walter get up on the ski slope under three or four feet of snow? There are quite a few questions I'd like to have answered."

"Yes, Mr. Ross." Harper took a deep breath. "All I can do is try. I've thought about it."

"I'm sure you have."

Harper swallowed. "They haven't said how he was killed. Maybe if there's an inquest, or maybe it'll be in the papers. They ran a picture of him—"

"I saw."

"Look, Mr. Ross—"

"No," Ross said. "It's the other way around. You look, and listen. Walter was carrying a bundle. It's gone. I want to know who got it. Do we have competition? I want answers." He paused. "And if you can't supply them, Pauley, then we'll get someone in who can." His voice had not risen.

Harper swallowed again. "We don't have competition, Mr. Ross, not really. There's a faggot who runs a shop and does a little business on the side. But he's been told, and he'll behave himself."

"Three deaths, Pauley. That isn't good."

"No, Mr. Ross."

"Deaths are bad for business."

"Yes, Mr. Ross."

"We don't want any more deaths. Is that clear?"

Harper nodded in silence, not trusting himself to speak. He picked up his glass and drank deep. The bourbon tasted no better than before. He set the glass down carefully.

"We will be here a week," Ross said. "Within that time I want answers. Is that clear?" Slight emphasis on the last sentence demanded answer.

"Yes, Mr. Ross."

For the first time Ross picked up his own glass, sniffed it, drank, set it down gently. "Now, Pauley," he said, "about the land development. How is it going?"

In the change of subject there was infinite relief, reprieve. "It's going to be all right. It's going to be fine. Some of the locals are," Harper even managed a smile, "dragging their feet a little, but they'll come around.

There's a high-yellow girl, anthropologist, well thought of. Her endorsement would carry a lot of weight.''

"Then get her endorsement, Pauley."

"Yes, Mr. Ross."

"However you have to," Ross said. "Sixteen thousand acres at three hundred dollars an acre is four million eight hundred thousand dollars, and that's just the beginning. Improvements, sales costs, legal costs, the well-drilling you wrote about—" Ross paused. "We want the investment to pay off."

"It will, Mr. Ross. It will."

Ross smiled. "It had better, Pauley. Now drink your drink. I want to watch Cindy's tennis lesson." He stood up. "Her backhand is weak, and I don't like that."

The skin-flick theatre was between a butcher shop and the State Employment Office. Its small marquee bore no film title, merely a permanent *XXX RATED XXX*, and a smaller ADULTS ONLY.

"Consenting adults, *sin duda,*" Tony said. "Isn't that the popular phrase?"

The ticket window was inside, next to the popcorn machine. The attendant was young and female, wearing a light, tight sweater and, obviously, no brassiere. "Oh, God," she said. "What is this, a raid?"

"Just some questions," Johnny said. "You've been here how long?"

"Long enough. Some of the jerk customers think I'm part of the show."

"Aren't you?" This was Tony, staring thoughtfully at her breasts.

50

The girl sighed wearily. "Okay. Ask your questions."

"I asked one," Johnny said. "Were you working here the first of the year?"

"Why?" The girl was wary now.

Johnny said nothing.

"Okay," the girl said presently. "I was here. I've been here since Thanksgiving. A girl has to work somewhere, doesn't she?"

Johnny took out the picture of Walter Wilson. "Do you remember this man?"

"That," the girl said, "is the guy in the paper, isn't it?" She shivered faintly. "Maybe I saw him. Why would I remember?" She squared her shoulders and thrust out her breasts aggressively. "You think I remember every guy who comes in?" She tried evasive tactics. "Why don't you ask that old crow who runs the junk shop across the way? She watches everybody who comes in."

"I've talked with her," Johnny said. "She tells me this man came here four or five times in the afternoons, and one day he came here twice." He watched the girl steadily.

The girl hesitated. Then, "Oh, hell, yes, I remember him. We were running a flick about girl camps in Hitler Germany, and I wondered what scene it was that turned this guy on so he came back to see it again. There was whipping, and straight balling, and a dyke scene—" She shook her head. "I never did find out because I never saw him again. He must have sneaked out the alley door because when I went up to the booth to set up the projector again, I looked, and there wasn't anybody in the seats.''

Tony was watching Johnny's face. It showed nothing. Johnny said, ''There had been other—customers?''

''Sure.'' The girl even smiled. ''That was a good flick. The girls weren't bad in it, not like some of the dogs they show that wouldn't turn anybody on no matter what they did.'' She smiled again. ''I didn't mind watching that one myself. It kind of, you know, got to me, parts of it. That was why I wondered about him.'' She pointed at the picture.

Johnny said, ''You were here alone?''

''For the first two shows. That was all we ran that day. Joe, he owns the joint, he came in while I was setting up the projector for the third showing, and he said it was snowing so hard there was no sense staying open any longer, all anybody was thinking of was getting home if they could, so I said okay with me and left. Joe closed up.''

Johnny said, ''Joe who?''

''Joe Warren,'' Tony said. ''I know him. He runs that rental place. You know, power mowers and floor waxers and wheelbarrows. You name it.'' He looked at the girl, who nodded.

''That's him,'' the girl said.

''I think,'' Johnny said, ''that we'll take a look inside.''

''Help yourself,'' the girl said. She seemed relieved that the question-and-answer ordeal was over.

Inside the theatre it was dark; that was the first thing that struck you. The light from the small projector cast its colored shadows on the screen, and on the sound track a woman's voice moaned with a monotonous lack of conviction. Johnny and Tony stood at the head of the aisle and waited for their eyes to adjust. It took a little time.

Gradually shapes appeared. Johnny counted an audience of six, widely spaced. Automatically he counted the seats: ten rows of eight seats each, a hopeful capacity of eighty. Beside the screen there was a closed door; undoubtedly the one the girl had mentioned that led to the alley. But Johnny doubted that Wilson had gone out that way, as the girl assumed, under his own power.

Tony was watching the screen. *"Madre de Dios,"* he said. "What will they think of next?"

Johnny studied the naked figures of two women and a man writhing in tangled confusion. He shook his head. "I think they've already outmaneuvered themselves," he said, and led the way back to the foyer. To the girl he said, "When you're setting up the projector for a new showing, do you turn on the house lights?"

"Not very bright." The girl seemed totally relaxed now. She smiled easily. "Our customers don't like too much light." She paused, and the smile spread. "Seen all you want?"

"Ample."

The girl nodded understandingly. "I know what you mean. We take what we can get. Some flicks are better than others, and this isn't one of the good ones. Sorry about that."

Johnny led the way out into the bright sunlight where Tony blinked against the glare. "Like coming out of a

53

cave," he said, "a cave that stinks." He watched Johnny. "Where now?"

"Let's have a look at the alley."

There were trash cans and barrels. A dog took fright at their approach and hurried around a nearby corner. Johnny looked thoughtfully at the closed theatre door. "It was snowing hard," he said.

"If it's the day I think it was," Tony said, "it was snowing to beat hell. Time it finished, we had near two feet on the level here in town, let alone drifts. Nothing moved."

"Something did," Johnny said, and the germ of an idea began to grow. "Let's go see Joe Warren."

He was a big man, this Joe Warren, tall as Tony Lopez, and broader. "Judy called from the theatre," he said. "She said you'd be around. Why?"

Around them were power tools and portable generators, wheelbarrows and mechanical hoists, three cement mixers side by side, a rack of chain saws . . . Johnny took his time looking at everything. He said at last, "The day of the big January snow, remember?" He was looking straight at Warren now.

"I guess so," Warren said. "It was a mess."

"You went to the theatre," Johnny said, "and told the girl there was no need to stay open. Is that right?"

"She's a good kid," Warren said, "and she lives out of town. I figured she'd better get home while she could." He paused. "So?"

"So you closed up," Johnny said.

"I don't know why you're interested," Warren said, "but that's right. It doesn't take much. Empty the till. Turn off the lights. Lock the doors." He shrugged.

"Not quite," Johnny said. He was guessing, but the feeling was strong that this was how it had been. "There was something a little out of the ordinary that afternoon, wasn't there?"

Tony Lopez opened his mouth and then closed it again in silence.

"Like what?" Warren said.

Nothing changed in Johnny's voice. "Like a dead man, lying on his side between two rows of seats. The girl hadn't seen him from the projection booth. Neither had anybody else, except the man who killed him, and he had already gone."

"Come on!" Warren said. "You guys—"

Johnny held out the picture of Walter Wilson. "This is the man. We found him up on the ski slope where he'd been since that big snow."

"And how did he get there?" Warren said. "Did he fly?"

Johnny looked around the large store, then back at Warren again. "In winter," he said, "you rent snowmobiles, no?"

Tony Lopez said softly, "Jesus Christ."

Warren said overloud, "So I rent snowmobiles, so what? What does that mean, goddam it? What—?"

"The dead man was there," Johnny said. "The girl had gone. Nobody was around." He paused, thinking how it had to have been, sure now that he had it right. "You own a skin-flick theatre, you're walking on thin ice. Miss McDade—"

"That snoopy goddam old fart," Warren said.

"There are other people in town," Johnny said, "who don't like porno films. They'd love an excuse to

55

see you shut down. A dead man in your theatre might just be that excuse.'' He was silent, waiting.

Warren said, his voice quiet now, ''You're doing the talking.''

''The snow was your chance,'' Johnny said. ''And one of your snowmobiles was the thing. Wilson wasn't too big for you to handle, and the ski basin isn't all that far away. With any luck, the body would be buried so deep by the time the snow ended that it wouldn't even be found until spring. Which is precisely what happened.''

There was silence. Warren studied Johnny's face. ''You trying to hang a murder on me?''

''No,'' Johnny said. ''You didn't kill him. I'll bet on that. It was a professional job. You panicked and moved him, that's all I'm saying. And for some cooperation I might even forget that you did that.''

There was a long silence this time. Warren said at last, ''Might?''

''If you level with me,'' Johnny said. ''For example, was he wearing a belt when you found him?''

''He—'' Warren stopped. He shook his head. ''Tricky bastard, aren't you?''

''You said it,'' Tony said. He was grinning now. *''Muy tricudo,* as a friend of mine says.''

Johnny said, ''Was he wearing a belt?''

Warren seemed to swell. ''How the hell do I know if he was wearing a belt?'' he shouted. ''I didn't undress him. He was wearing a raincoat and there was a hat on the floor near him.'' He was breathing hard. ''I didn't even see him at first, and then I did, and I thought, Jesus Christ, this is going to blow it for sure.

56

That old fart McDade and others like her would just love to get me by the balls for showing films their husbands like to see, just making a buck.'' He stopped, and his voice suddenly turned quiet again. ''Okay,'' he said. ''I hauled the little bastard out from the seats, came around here and got a snowmobile, and loaded him into it in the alley. It was snowing to beat hell; you couldn't see fifteen feet. So I headed for the ski basin, and that's where I dumped him, where nobody'd see me.'' He paused. ''For all I knew, he'd had a heart attack. I didn't see any blood. But I sure as hell didn't want him found in my place however he got dead.''

''He was wearing a gun in a hideaway holster,'' Johnny said. ''Did you know that?'' Because if you did, he thought, you would also have known whether he was wearing a belt or not. He waited.

''I told you,'' Warren said. ''I didn't undress him. All I wanted was to get rid of him.'' It held the ring of truth.

6

"So that, chica," Johnny said, "is where we are now."
He and Cassie were sitting in front of the corner fireplace in Cassie's house. Burning piñon logs gave off
their clean fragrance. Chico lay quiet at their feet, staring into the flames.

"And what do you think?" Cassie said. She had seen
it before, but always she was impressed by this man's
deductions that were worked out as carefully as her own
when, with infinite patience, she juxtaposed in time the
findings in a dig. "Is Warren telling the truth?"

"I think so," Johnny's voice was quiet, relaxed. "I
think the belt was already gone when Warren found
him. I think it was probably a money belt and that may
well have been the reason for the hit." He paused.
"Remember, his wallet was gone too. Somebody
wanted him dead, and didn't want him identified right
away."

Despite the fire Cassie shivered. "But he couldn't
have counted on Warren and a snowmobile."

"No," Johnny said. "He played it lucky. And I

wouldn't be surprised if he wondered what had happened when the body didn't turn up." Another thoughtful pause. "And now that it has, he's maybe looking in every direction at once to see who buried it and knows more than he's said so far. And why."

Newton Berry had cleaned up his shop, rescued what *cosas* he could, and reluctantly, almost tearfully, discarded those that were totally worthless. The blast damage to walls, fireplace, and windows had been repaired. The smell of incense hid the ugly odor of the explosion. But the scars on Berry's psyche remained, angry and unhealed.

He had customers this afternoon, a Mr. and Mrs. Ross, staying out at the Lodge, obviously well-heeled. That light fur stole Mrs. Ross wore against the spring chill would be proof of solvency in any company. With them was their slim, teenage daughter, a smiling child.

Berry was apologetic. "I'm afraid my stock at the moment isn't quite up to par. A dreadful accident, an explosion." He spread his hands helplessly. "But I do have some rather nice things that managed to survive the holocaust." He produced a smile.

Ross said pleasantly, "Why don't you two just look around?" And then, to Berry, "Explosion? Too bad. A gas leak?"

Berry shook his head. He glanced around. The women were out of earshot. "I'm afraid not," Berry said. "It seems to have been of all things a bomb." Should he have said that? He didn't know. But Mr. Ross did not seem the kind of man to take fright easily, and there was even the possibility that Mr. Ross's sympathies might be aroused.

Mr. Ross remained singularly unimpressed. "Competition," he said, "must be rough in your business." He smiled at Berry. The smile did not reach the shiny, brown, steady eyes. "I'll look around too, if I may," Ross said.

They bought. For a few unpleasant moments Berry entertained the fearful notion that Mr. and Mrs. Ross had come, not to see his shop, but solely to look him over; but, he told himself, they would hardly have carried mere reconnaissance to the length of buying a six hundred and fifty dollar, hand-woven Indian rug, and he breathed easier. "It is a lovely thing, isn't it," he said. "Such divine composition. Too many people, even otherwise knowledgeable people, fail to recognize the superb craftsmanship and the simply out-of-this-world imagery the Southwest Indian is capable of. A great pity."

Mrs. Ross said, "It will look lovely in your library, Peter."

The girl said, "It's neat, Daddy."

Ross's face and voice showed nothing. "You'll be good enough to ship it for us? I'll write you a check." He did, and held it out. "The address is there," he said. Was there anything behind the words, the tone, the quiet eyes? Berry could not be sure. "And I hope you have no more—trouble," Ross said.

"I certainly hope not too," Berry said. And then, with an assurance he did not feel, "I'm sure I won't."

Ross nodded. "Good," he said, and that was all. To his wife and daughter, "I think lunch now."

The girl said, "You promised us some of that groovy Mexican food, Daddy."

"Mexican food it will be." A family man, devoted to his womenfolk.

Then why, Berry asked himself as he watched them walk away, did he find himself trembling, and the palms of his hands a trifle damp? As it had been when he talked with that frightening part-Apache creature, the police lieutenant? And for the same reason. Because both men had given the unmistakable impression that they had stripped him bare, and actually *ogled* his poor secrets. He closed the shop and went straight home for a stiff drink and a soothing cup of tea.

The narcotics man, whose name was Snyder, sat in Johnny's office. "I doubt if I can tell you anything you don't already know," he said. "For a long time the main source of raw opium has been the poppy fields of Turkey. The usual route has been into the south of France where in God only knows how many little labs or factories, heroin is extracted. From there—" Snyder's shrug was both angry and helpless. "Other countries are having their problems now too, but we remain the principal market. What you get here probably comes up from Mexico. Sometimes we can stop it; sometimes we can't. That isn't much help, is it?"

"I wasn't expecting miracles," Johnny said. Long ago he had learned that you followed trail after trail which turned out to be false because, occasionally, a false trail cut another that did lead somewhere, and you could then follow the new scent. "I'm running in circles with my nose to the ground," he said, and showed the white teeth in a sudden smile, "and if that makes a pretty funny picture in your mind, why, maybe it is, at that.'' The smile was gone. ''From Turkey to France to Mexico to the U.S.,'' he said, ''does that argue a single organization, or is it a kind of seller-to-buyer chain?''

''We think both,'' Snyder said. ''Some operations, particularly big ones, argue organization that plans every step of the way. Others are probably just what you say, seller to buyer who in turn sells to another buyer farther on.''

Johnny leaned back in his chair and listened to his inaudible voices. It amused him that an Anglo shrink would probably say it was merely his subconscious bubbling up ideas. Same thing, no? ''Three deaths here,'' he said. ''All from bad heroin.'' He paused. ''Does that suggest organization?''

Snyder thought about it. ''Probably not. The pros are businessmen, and deaths, particularly from a bad product, are bad for business.''

Johnny had thought as much. The inaudible voices were still talking. ''What would happen,'' he said, ''if in an organization's territory, some small operator came up with bad heroin that caused some deaths?''

Again Snyder took his time. He said at last, ''I don't think I would like to be in the small operator's shoes. I think something might land on him pretty hard.''

And that, too, was as Johnny had thought. He nodded. ''Now another direction,'' he said, and tapped the picture of Walter Wilson that lay on his desk. ''You've seen him. We have no make on him, no prints, no record. When he was found he was dressed in . . .'' He read the list of clothing from Saul Pentland's report.

"To me," Johnny said, "that just adds up to Eastern flatland dude. Does it mean anything more to you?"

Snyder looked puzzled. "I don't get the question."

"Well," Johnny said, "consider the clothing. Consider the man. There's nothing distinctive about him, no calluses, nothing to indicate that he worked with his hands at all, or that he wore glasses, or that he spent a lot of time in the sun in swim trunks or stayed out of the sun entirely—do you see what I mean? Just an ordinary fellow you'd find riding a commuter train." He paused. "Except that he wore a hideaway holster and a lightweight five-shot thirty-eight with a two-inch barrel." He watched Snyder's eyebrows rise. "And," Johnny said, "when we found him he wasn't wearing a belt and his pants would have fallen off without one, and maybe the kind of belt he no longer had was a money belt. Just guesswork, but—" He stopped.

"I'm beginning to see what you mean," Snyder said. "Is there more?"

"He was killed," Johnny said, "by a knife, or maybe even an ice pick, stuck into his spinal cord just here." He touched the back of his neck. "While he was sitting in a porno movie house." He sat silent then, waiting with bone-bred patience.

Snyder saw the direction clearly now, and could admire the mind that had pointed the way. "You're asking, in effect," he said, "what the table of organization looks like in one of the big operations." He shook his head. "Not quite like the Army, or General Motors; there isn't a chart you can go to."

"But there are certain jobs." Johnny smiled suddenly again. "I'm, like I said, running in circles with my nose to the ground. I'm hoping to cut a new trail by what you tell me, but I don't want to put words in your mouth that might start me in a wrong direction. Maybe I'm already clear off the reservation. I don't know. I'm hoping you can tell me.''

Snyder said slowly, ''What you're asking is, considering his clothes, no record, no signs of occupation, plus the handgun and the belt that's missing, does Wilson seem to me to fit one of the jobs a big organization would have?'' He nodded. ''Reasonable question, but all I can do is guess at the answer.''

''I'll listen to anything,'' Johnny said.

In Snyder's experience, there were few who would, but he had an idea this one meant what he said, and suddenly he wanted very much to help. ''All right,'' he said, ''let's cut out a couple of jobs he doesn't fit. He wouldn't be top echelon. They don't carry guns. And they don't carry enough cash, if that's what was in the belt, to make it worth what sounds like a professional hit. They carry credit cards, maybe a few loose checks, and tipping money.''

So far, so good, Johnny thought. Those inaudible voices sometimes had good ideas. ''Scratch top echelon,'' he said.

''There are the muscle men,'' Snyder said, ''the enforcers, but I think we can scratch that job for him, too. They don't carry a lot of cash, either; but, maybe even more important, they're usually good at their jobs, and I don't see one sitting still in a movie house while somebody sticks a shiv into his spinal cord.''

Better and better, Johnny thought. ''We're clearing out the underbrush,'' he said, ''and even if that doesn't give us a clear look at what he was and what he was doing, at least we won't have to waste time on what we've thrown out.''

Snyder settled deeper into his chair. ''There have to be pushers,'' he said, ''but they don't fit, either. A pusher here in Santo Cristo in the clothes he was wearing would stand out like the Pan Am Building in the desert.''

Johnny thought of Ruben Martinez, the dead boy, and could only agree. The Ruben Martinezes were the customers, and they would not be dealing with anyone as conspicuous as Walter Wilson. He nodded.

''A step up from the pusher,'' Snyder said, ''would be a distributor with a territory.'' He paused. ''That would be a possibility—except, again, for the way he was dressed. Suppose you have a distributor covering, say, two, three states here in the Southwest. He'd be a damn fool if he didn't blend a little more into the landscape than your dead Eastern dude.'' He studied Johnny's face. ''What are you thinking?''

''A picture I saw once,'' Johnny said, ''of Calvin Coolidge in a feather headdress. All he looked like was Calvin Coolidge in a feather headdress. I can't see Wilson blending into this landscape no matter what clothes you put on him.''

Snyder was smiling and nodding. ''So we come to what you've probably thought all along, don't we?'' He had been led, but he felt no resentment, merely wonder that it was now so clear. ''The distributor sells to the pusher and collects. But somebody also collects from the distributors, somebody from what you might call the home office, somebody who might very well wear a money belt and a handgun to protect it, and who might make contact in a porno movie house.'' He nodded again. Simple enough when you looked right at it. "Is that what you wanted me to say?''

Johnny nodded. The fresh trail was now established. Where it would lead, he had no idea, but he could stop going in circles.

"The question,'' Snyder said, "is who would dare make a hit, a professional hit, on a collector from the home office?'' He paused. "Not a distributor on his own unless he was itching for more trouble than he was likely to survive, that's for sure.''

"On his own,'' Johnny said. "Spell that one out.''

Snyder spread his hands. "All we know for sure most times is what we see coming to the surface. We don't see the brawling that may go on within the organization, one branch, one family, maybe thinking it's been getting the short end of the stick, and wanting to expand its operations. Then maybe a direct challenge, an attempted takeover that may or may not succeed. Knock over the home office's collector, show that the people behind him can't protect him, make your move and defy them to do anything about it.'' He paused. His face and his voice were solemn. "Guesswork,'' he said.

"That's all we have,'' Johnny said.

7

The Santo Cristo police blotter for that Saturday recorded:

A shoplifter reported by Sears;

Gunshots on Mesa Drive;

Fights reported at El Matador Drive-In, Pasatiempo Theatre, and Dave's Bar & Grill;

Broken windows at La Paloma fabric center, Joe's Liquor Store, and the Santo Cristo High School gymnasium;

A breaking and entering on Arroyo Road;

A dog bite in the Santo Cristo Plaza;

Motor vehicle accidents on Cadiz Street, San José Drive, Avenida Collegio, and Bryce Lane.

What the police blotter did not record was the little drama involving María Victoria Sanchez and Ruth Rogers, both eighteen, and therefore open to report in public records. It came about this way:

There was a point of land overlooking Arroyo Hondo

which the youth of Santo Cristo had pre-empted for their own purposes. They called it, from the movie title: Planet of the Apes; or, for short: Apes. The point was reached by a quarter of a mile of wheel tracks leading out across grama and ring grass from Hondo Road. It was from one of the four houses along the two miles of Hondo Road that the telephone call came to police headquarters. The duty sergeant turned it over to Tony Lopez.

"Look," the male, Anglo, puzzled voice said, "I'm not drunk, and I don't think I've lost my marbles, but there are a couple of buck-naked chicks romping around out here, and, well, my wife says something ought to be done about it." Pause for breath. "My name is Sanders and I live on Hondo Road right across from that, you know, that point where kids drive to do—well, you name it, and from the looks of things out there they do it."

"I know the point, Mr. Sanders," Tony said.

"But there's no car. I went out to see. Just the two naked chicks dodging around in the bushes." Another pause. "Look, I'm not making this up."

"We'll look into it, Mr. Sanders," Tony said. "Thank you for calling."

Johnny was off duty that day, but he stopped in anyway, driven by he knew not what compulsive itch to talk about what Snyder the narco had clarified for him. He caught Tony just hanging up the phone.

"Maybe," Tony said, "you'd better chaperone me, amigo. This is some kind of mission for a single guy." He explained, and watched Johnny's amusement.

"You? Afraid?" Johnny said. "Okay, I'll come along

and hold your hand." He paused. "Hands," he said. "We'll take a sedan. And a couple of blankets. Just in case."

Sanders was waiting where the wheel tracks took off from the road. He pointed. "Out yonder, and they can't have gone anywhere because I've been watching. And it's too steep to go down into the arroyo."

"Okay," Johnny said. "Thanks."

"I'd give you a hand," Sanders said, "but my wife would raise hell." He watched wistfully as the police sedan drove off and disappeared over a little rise.

The view from the point was spectacular. Two hundred feet below a small stream meandered amongst willows and an occasional cottonwood. To the south where the arroyo widened, its sloping sides framed the solid bulk of Cloud Mesa forty miles away. The sky was clear, deep blue and bright; the air was tonic. And there were two naked girls trying inadequately to hide behind a single piñon tree, arms across breasts and hands at pubic areas in the traditional attitude.

Johnny got out of the sedan with the two blankets. "Here." He tossed them one at a time, and the girls snatched them up and enveloped themselves.

The Anglo girl said, "Jesus, it would have to be fuzz."

The Spanish girl said, "I don't care who it is. Not any more."

And Tony, smiling, said, "That's the spirit, *guapa*. Play it as it comes." He held the rear door of the sedan with a bow and a flourish.

Sanders was still standing on Hondo Road as they drove out. He watched in silence, unmoving.

"The old goat," the Anglo girl said. "He came all the way out for a good look."

"Claro," the Spanish girl said. "What else would he do after he saw us?"

"He has a wife," Tony said. "She disapproves of naked shenanigans."

The Anglo girl said, "I suppose you're going to take us in?"

"I think," Johnny said, "that a few questions are in order, no?"

"You going to book us? We didn't do anything. It was those—bastards."

"Who?" Johnny said.

The Spanish girl said quickly, *"No importa.* Their names do not matter." She looked at her friend. "You hear?"

The Anglo girl shrugged. "Their fault."

"No." The Spanish girl was firm. "It was a *chiste,* a joke."

"Some joke."

"We asked for it, no?"

They sat in Johnny's office, the door closed. María Victoria said, "You tell, or do I?" And when Ruth sat silent, María Victoria launched into the tale.

There were these guys, three of them, and their names didn't matter. What they wanted wasn't what Johnny probably thought, although neither María Victoria nor Ruth had been all that sure at first. It was simple, really; what the guys wanted was to take pictures like, you know, in *Playboy?* Anything wrong with that?

Given the current attitudes of society toward nudity

70

and, indeed, sex, Johnny thought, maybe it made some kind of sense. Maybe it didn't, too. He decided that as a moralizer he was a good cop. "Go on," he said.

Well, the guys had made the proposition, and they were going to pay the girls. You know, models, they get paid, don't they? And all the artists and photographers here in Santo Cristo, it's the same thing they do, isn't it? What they call figure studies? So, okay. After an amount of I-will-if-you-will between the girls, the decision to pose was made. After all, *two* girls, not just one, it was, you know, safer that way.

Tony Lopez shook his head in slow wonder. "In my day, *guapa*—" he began. He stopped. Johnny was watching him with amusement. "I know," Tony said slowly, sadly. "I'm over thirty and that changes everything. Go on."

Well, that was all there was to it. The guys had really been having them on. You know, a *chiste*, a joke. Soon as the girls had stripped and were posed against a piñon tree, the guys jumped in the car and took off.

"With our clothes," Ruth said, "and laughing to beat hell. How about that? We might have known. They—"

María Victoria said sharply, "No names!"

"Tell me why," Johnny said.

María Victoria shrugged. "What good would it do? Just make a stink and show us up for fools." She paused. "Which we are."

Ruth said, "You going to book us? And if so, for what?"

"There are statutes," Tony said, "against walking around bare-assed." He looked at Johnny.

71

"I don't see any point," Johnny said, and got a long appraising look from María Victoria.

"Maybe," she said slowly, even reluctantly, "you aren't quite the bastard you're supposed to be."

"You drive them home," Johnny said to Tony. "They can do their own explaining. And don't forget to bring the blankets back." He looked then at María Victoria. "Next time you get the itch to pose in the nude—" he began.

"No way," María Victoria said.

Both girls rode in the rear seat of the police car. Ruth said, "Your folks will be home?"

"Naturally." In the mirror Tony saw María Victoria's smile at the ingenuousness of the question. "Father, mother, seven brothers and sisters," she said, "and the *abuela,* the grandmother. You think the house is ever empty?"

Ruth was silent, thoughtful. "Look, fuzz," she said to Tony, "how about a telephone? Maybe I can get somebody to bring us some clothes. And then," she said to María Victoria, "we can pretend we switched, and—"

"You heard the man," Tony said. "He said to drive you home and let you do your explaining there."

"Screw him." Pause. "And you too. You fuzz are all alike, just waiting for a chance to get somebody in trouble."

Tony had heard it before. In the normal course of things, he thought, he would hear it perhaps a thousand times again before he retired. He shrugged and glanced again in the mirror. What he saw on María Victoria's face changed things. He said in rapid Spanish, "What are you thinking, chica?"

The girl shook her head in stubborn silence.

Ruth said, "What'd he ask you?"

Another shake of the dark head.

"Maybe," Tony said, in Spanish still, "I can guess." He wasn't normally this perceptive, he thought; maybe some of that Indian's goddam prescience had rubbed off on him, or something, but it was clear enough in his mind, and the more he thought about it, the better he liked it. "Because," he said, "you and I were taught the same things, *verdad?*"

The girl sat straight and unyielding, silent. Only her eyes, watching his in the mirror, showed comprehension.

Ruth said, "What's he saying? He trying to con you into something?"

"Ignore her," Tony said. "There are good Anglos and bad Anglos, and she is a pig. You are María Victoria Sanchez. I know your family. When you were young you were taught that there was right and there was wrong, and if no one else saw, God still knew when you did wrong, and punishment would come some day some way, there was no escaping it."

"Goddam you," Ruth said, "stop it! Or talk English!"

"From ones like her," Tony said unperturbed in Spanish still, "you learned other ways, easy ways. Smoke, drink, lie. Display your nakedness and boys will pay you." He took one hand from the steering wheel and popped his fingers. "Nothing. *Nada y nada por nada.*" He paused, and his voice altered. "But that is not how your family will see it. They will be angry, and ashamed, and so you know that it is not nothing, it is something wrong that you have done, as you knew all along that it was. And you will be punished, because that is the way it is and has always been. And you are even glad that you will be punished, that I will not allow you to telephone and tell lies to your friends, your family. Instead you will tell your family the truth. And they will be angry, and ashamed, and there will be punishment—but you will feel better." Tony paused. "Is that not so, María Victoria?"

There was a long silence. The girl said at last, in Spanish, "You sound like my father."

"I am honored," Tony said.

Ruth said, resignation clear, "Okay, fuzz, stop here."

Tony looked at the expanse of adobe wall, the wrought ironwork of the gate, the tended flower garden, and the sprawling house that shrieked of affluence. He said, in English now, "This is where you live?"

"What if it is?"

Tony turned. To María Victoria, in Spanish again, "This is her house?"

"Sí." The voice was quiet, subdued.

"Okay," Tony said and released the rear door. "Out you get. I'll come back for the blanket." He paused. "Good luck."

Ruth's smile was scornful. "Thanks for nothing, you bastard." She tossed her head as she walked to the gate.

At the Sanchez house, no adobe wall, no wrought iron gate, three small children playing amongst four

74

dogs in the bare front yard, Tony released the rear door again. "Good luck," he said, and watched María Victoria get out.

She stood quietly for a moment studying him. Then, "Thank you, *señor.*" She walked like a queen, Tony thought, past the small children and the dogs, up the steps, the blanket held tight around her.

Back at headquarters, perched on the corner of Johnny's desk, "You ought to have heard me, amigo," Tony said. He shook his head, smiling at the spectacle of himself preaching. "I must have sounded like a priest."

"Probably." Johnny nodded. "But don't knock it."

The telephone call reached Johnny late that evening at Cassie's house. "I was told to call here, *señor.*" In Spanish. "I am María Victoria Sanchez."

"I remember you well." Johnny's voice was gentle. "I hope your punishment was not too severe."

"No importa." There was a pause. The girl had been crying, and perhaps still was; her voice was unsteady. "May I talk to you, *señor?*"

"About what, María Victoria?"

There was a long pause this time, and audible sniffling. Then, "Ruben Martinez," the girl said. "He and I—" The voice stopped. At last it resumed. "We were going to speak of marriage, *señor,* after he—broke his habit, and found a job."

"I see." Johnny spoke quietly, feeling his way with care. "You wish to tell me what, María Victoria?"

"Please, *señor.* You will meet me? I can tell you where Ruben got—what he thought he had to have—" Pause. "—that killed him."

Johnny blinked. "I will meet you," he said. "Tell me where and when."

He listened carefully, hung up and stood looking at Cassie. "There are days," he said, "when it doesn't pay to get out of bed. Other days—" He shook his head in wonder. "Tony got to her, somehow."

"Or you did," Cassie said. She watched him walk to the door, hesitate, and then smile back into the room before he walked out into the night.

8

The road was well within the city limits, but it was dirt and it had been a long time since the grader had come through; Johnny's pick-up bounced and jostled. At the intersection he slowed, dimmed his lights, and stopped. The girl was no more than a shadow slipping out of darkness and into the cab beside him. They drove off.

"I hope I am doing what is right, *señor.*"

So do I, Johnny thought. Aloud he said, "You are."

"What happened today—" The girl was silent.

"It is best forgotten."

"No, *señor.*" The girl's voice was firm. "It is to be remembered." Pause. "Did you ever dream that you were naked and you tried to hide but there was no hiding place?" She had turned to look at the dim blur of Johnny's face. "Because that was how it was today, like a bad dream, but it was real. Ruth was angry, but I was only—ashamed."

There was silence between them. Johnny drove slowly, keeping to unlighted streets while he waited for the girl to speak. It was, he told himself, no time for questioning. The girl was poised on the edge of conscience and a wrong word could ruin everything.

At last she spoke. "Ruben," she said, and turned again to look at Johnny's face. "He was a—good boy, *señor.*"

"He was a brave man," Johnny said.

"You know about that? His medal?" Her voice was pleased. "I have it. He gave it to me. After he broke his habit, he said, and we could be married, then the medal would be ours. It was our engagement gift. He had no money to buy a ring."

Johnny said gently, "He had spent his money, his Army pay?"

"Heroin is expensive, *señor.* In Viet Nam it was cheap."

True enough. How many had found out the same? And what was there to say that would not sound like a moralistic TV commercial? Worse, Johnny could almost feel the girl slipping away from him. "María Victoria," he said, "listen to me. All heroin is bad. But what killed your Ruben was poison. He was the third to die from it. Whether there will be more, I don't know." He paused. "It may depend on you."

There was silence. Then, "That is not fair, *señor.*"

"Fair has nothing to do with it." Johnny's voice was no longer gentle. "It isn't fair that your Ruben is dead. It isn't fair that the others are dead. It isn't fair that some men steal and cheat and kill and it isn't fair that others lie to protect them." He paused. "Or remain silent when they could talk. That is a kind of lying too, María Victoria." Now he was the one who preached, and it annoyed him that he found it necessary. He decided that the sermon was ended.

The girl was silent for a time. She said at last, "Will you tell me, *señor,* why you did not arrest us today, put down in the record what we had done? Are there not laws against nakedness?"

"There are," Johnny said. "And I'm supposed to enforce the laws. But what you had done—" He shook his head, almost angry with himself now. "It wasn't that important. Not these days. Not—"

"I think it was something else," the girl said. "I think it was because you are a kind man and you did not want to hurt us. Thank you, *señor.*"

It was, Johnny thought, the first time that anybody had ever called him a kind man, and he did not know whether to laugh or resent it. Cassie, he thought, would be amused at his dilemma. She would—"What did you say?" He turned to look at the girl.

She was sitting quiet, contained, her hands folded now in her lap. She seemed at ease, at peace. "The name of the man, *señor,* is Waldo. His last name I do not know. He works at the motel near the Alameda—"

"The Mid-Towner," Johnny said. Where Walter Wilson had stayed, but left no record, no luggage. Coincidence? "Do you know this man, María Victoria?"

"No, *señor.* Ruben told me his name, that was all."

Pure hearsay, Johnny thought; no matter, it was a direction. "Did Ruben mention other names?"

"I do not remember any."

"Walter Wilson?"

"I do not remember the name, *señor.*" Quietly, almost unobtrusively, the girl began to cry. Her words came indistinctly, oddly spaced with emotion. "Ruben was not a bad boy, *señor*. If he had not—died, he would have broken the habit, I know it, and we would have been married." She was silent. Then, "A Mass was said for his soul, *señor*, but because he died doing wrong—" She was silent again.

And what do I say to that? Johnny asked himself, and found no satisfactory answer. But he had to try. "What Ruben did," he said, "buying heroin, taking it, was against the law, just as what you did today was against the law. But there are greater offenses and smaller offenses, and the greater offense is with the one who sells the heroin, this Waldo, or those who are behind him." His voice took on an edge. "May they roast in hell, María Victoria, not your Ruben whose only offense was weakness." Not quite true, but near enough.

There was a long silence. Then, "Thank you, *señor*."

"I will take you back now," Johnny said.

He slowed at the same dark intersection, stopped. The girl started to open the door. "A moment," Johnny said. "Listen to me carefully. What you have done in telling me the man's name is right. But you are not to say any more about it; you are not to say that you have even seen me. Do you understand?"

"Sí, señor."

Did she really comprehend the reason? Johnny could not be sure. "I don't want to frighten you, María Victoria, but—"

"I understand." The girl's voice was calm. "It is well known what happens to those who go to the police.'' She opened the door, stepped out, closed the door again. Her face was a pale blur in the window opening. ''I knew when I telephoned you that I might get in trouble,'' she said, ''but I thought of Ruben, and of what happened today, what you said, and what the other one said.'' Pause. ''I cannot live in shame, *señor.*'' She was gone.

Johnny drove slowly back to the house on Arroyo Road. The outside light was on, and inside he could hear Chico barking a welcome. He was expected, wanted, and there was the wonder. Life was filled with surprises, which was a cliché if he had ever heard one. As he got out of the pick-up and started for the house, the door opened and Cassie appeared, smiling. ''Welcome back,'' Cassie said.

''To your house.'' Now why had he said that?

Cassie's smile was unchanged. *''Es tu casa, también,''* she said. It is thy house too. She held the door wide, and Chico rushed out to caper in delight.

Paul Harper sat again in Cassie's office. ''I'd like to start over, doctor,'' he said, and smiled. ''We can use your advice. Anthropology is your field, and this is your country. We can use your knowledge of both. Anthropology covers man and his environment, as well as his social relationships, doesn't it?''

True enough. Cassie decided that Paul Harper had done his research well. She said as much.

''I like to know what I'm getting into,'' Harper said. ''It's as simple as that, doctor. We are going to spend a great deal of money on this project, and we want it to be spent wisely. Someone like yourself in on the planning can save us from mistakes that might otherwise turn out to be very expensive.''

It made a kind of sense, Cassie thought, and wondered at the strong reluctance she felt. "I'm going to be very busy, Mr. Harper,'' she said. "We're opening a new dig south of town as soon as the weather lets us, and I don't think that will be very long. Then—''

"This is a rather special opportunity,'' Harper said. "You can benefit yourself, and the community.'' He was a salesman, with a salesman's sense of timing and knowledge of when to stop the pitch. "We can work out a consulting arrangement that wouldn't tie you down too much. For a fee, of course. Would you think one hundred dollars a day a reasonable figure, doctor?''

Cassie opened her mouth and shut it again in careful silence. On the floor at her feet Chico thumped his tail in inquiry. "I think that would be generous,'' Cassie said. "But I'm afraid—''

"Why don't you think about it?'' Harper said. He stood up. "Don't give me an answer now.'' He had a pleasing smile, neither fulsome nor hesitant. "In a few days, doctor, I'll come see you again.'' He left before Cassie could answer.

Cassie sat on in contemplation, booted legs outstretched. From time to time, idly, lovingly, she reached down to rub Chico's head or pull gently at the soft ears; the feel of his fur verified the fact of his presence, and that in itself was comfort, more than comfort.

All her life, until Chico and Johnny, she had been alone, conscious of, and resenting, her color, her health and physical beauty, and her brains and erudition because in combination they seemed to make any kind of fulfillment impossible. A white chick with her looks, body, and brains would be able to name her price and there would be no dearth of suitors to pay it. A brainy black chick, ugly as sin, with thick ankles and a bass voice, would be treated with respect purely on a professional level. Herself, with color, body, and looks but without brains would fare well on a physical plane. Or so it seemed. But the packaged product as it stood was never going to move off the shelf. Until Chico and Johnny; and how could she even begin to explain how she felt about that?

"A hundred little round dollars a day," she said to Chico. "An appealing thought, no?"

Chico thumped the floor with his tail.

But what would the money buy? There was the question. How much food could you eat? How many clothes could you wear? She had her house, her books, her music, her work, and Johnny. She looked down as Chico thumped the floor again. "And you," she said. "What more do we need?"

On the other hand, as who knew better than she, counting your blessings, although highly recommended as therapy by some authorities, was actually a very unsatisfying business. The fact of the matter was that the mere thought of one hundred dollars a day for consultation was very tempting indeed, as Harper had known it would be. Money, it seemed, had its own appeal, separate and distinct from its utility. She thought that another opinion would be of value, and Flora Hobbs immediately came to mind.

Flora owned and ran the local establishment known throughout the Southwest as Flora's House. No drunks were rolled, or even allowed; decorum was the watchword, and in Flora's place a man could count on peace, quiet, and an honest *quid pro quo*. Flora was a businesswoman.

Flora listened quietly in the parlor of the lovely old house that had once been a center of controversy. "Honey," she said when Cassie was done, "I've always been foursquare for taking the cash and letting the credit go. Where's the harm in taking the man's money in return for the sensible advice I'm sure you'll give him?"

"I don't know," Cassie said. "There are problems he doesn't recognize yet. Water is one."

"Then you get paid for pointing them out to him." Flora switched arguments. "Is there something wrong with the man?"

"I don't know that, either."

"You could check at the bank. You're well enough known to ask questions."

"I have." More and more it seemed that her reluctance was based on nothing. "His credit is practically unlimited. His Eastern references are sound."

"But you have a hunch." Flora saw deep. "Honey," she said, "is it possible that you're a little gun-shy? Like me?" Her gesture included the entire house. "What I run here isn't looked on with favor in some quarters, and that makes me something outside of the normal run of the mill."

"And I'm what I am," Cassie said. She nodded. The black girl and the whorehouse madam, pariahs together, she thought. We look at the whole world with suspicion. "Maybe that's it."

"Why don't you go see Ben Hart?" Flora said. "He'll give it to you straight."

The idea had been in Cassie's mind. She was delighted that Flora had thought of it too. "I think I will," she said.

9

The man's name was Waldo Davega. He worked nights at the Mid-Towner Motor Hotel as porter and desk assistant; days he worked at Bell's Supermarket pricing and stacking cans on shelves and, at need, doubling as a checker. Johnny would have tagged him as a slow, solid family man; certainly no run-of-the-mill pusher. It was puzzling.

"Ruben Martinez," Johnny said. "You knew him." They were standing in the storage area of the supermarket surrounded by crates of produce and questionable smells.

Waldo repeated the name slowly. "Maybe. I meet lots of people."

On a wild venture, "A man named Wilson, for example," Johnny said, "a guest in the motel a few months ago." Was there change in Waldo's eyes? "Walter Wilson," Johnny added.

"I don't know him." The words were too quick, too positive.

"Nobody seems to know him," Johnny said, "and

nobody seems to know what happened to his luggage, either.'' A new trail to follow, but in the meantime it was Ruben Martinez who concerned him. ''Ruben Martinez is dead,'' he said. ''So are two others. They all died recently from the same cause. Bad dope. The word is that you sold it.'' Seeing the man, he didn't for a moment believe it, but there was something there to be questioned or the girl María Victoria would not have known the man's name.

And Waldo was suddenly frightened; that much was plain. He seemed to be trying to look in all directions at once. ''I don't know anything about bad dope,'' he said. ''I don't know anything about any kind of dope. I don't know Ruben Martinez and I don't know Walter Wilson. Now I got work to do—''

''After you answer some questions,'' Johnny said. He paused for emphasis. ''Three dead men. Four, counting Wilson—''

''I tell you, I don't know him. Maybe I saw him a couple times, gave him change for the phone, took stuff he wanted put in the safe—''

''Hold it right there,'' Johnny said, and was silent for a little time, thinking how it might have been. ''What kind of stuff did he want in the safe?''

''I didn't say he did. I just said maybe. I—don't remember.''

''I think you'd better remember,'' Johnny said. He walked over to a lettuce crate and sat down. ''I'll tell you,'' he said conversationally. ''I've got all the time in the world. So have you.''

''I've got work to do.''

''You've got nothing to do until you start remembering some things." His thoughts were back on Walter Wilson now, for the moment abandoning Ruben Martinez. Or maybe the two were inextricably linked, and the more Johnny thought about it, the surer he was that it was so. "Walter Wilson wanted something put in the safe. We'll start there. What was it?"

Waldo's eyes jumped from place to place and found no solace. "I don't know. It—I mean, I don't remember."

Some you leaned on hard when you wanted information, Johnny thought; but some, like this one, could be frightened too easily into cataleptic immobility and silence. With these you used patience. "What was it?" he repeated. "Sooner or later you're going to tell me." He kept his eyes on Waldo's face. "I'm good at waiting, and I don't think you are."

Waldo hesitated and then took a deep breath. "It—it was just a package." He held his hands a few inches apart. "A little package. A—a box. It was wrapped."

Johnny nodded. "So far, so good," he said. "Now · for the rest of it. What happened to the box?" He watched Waldo's face begin to come apart like a photograph over-enlarged; and in his mind the quiet murmur of success arose. "What happened to it?" he said again.

Waldo's eyes rolled like those of a frightened horse. "It—I mean, he got it back. That's how it was. He came and asked for it and I gave it to him."

Johnny said very gently, "No. He didn't come back for anything. He was dead and buried in the snow. His little box was still in the safe, and his things were still in his room just the way he had left them.'' He paused. ''Try again, Waldo.''

Waldo said, ''Oh, God!'' He lowered himself slowly, uncertainly until his buttocks rested precariously on a melon crate. ''You're just going to get me in trouble.''

''No,'' Johnny said again. ''You've gotten yourself in trouble, and you're going in deeper if you're not careful. Just sit there for a few moments and think about it.''

''You—'' Waldo began. He stopped and shook his head in helpless silence.

''I think I know how it was,'' Johnny said. He took his time. ''Wilson was killed. I know how and I know where and I know how he got to the ski slope and under the snow.'' He paused. Waldo was watching him as if hypnotized. ''But you didn't know,'' Johnny said. ''Nobody at the motel knew until the next morning.'' He was guessing, but it almost had to be the way it was. ''When the maid went to clean Wilson's room, it was empty. Everything of his was gone, no?''

Waldo opened his mouth and shut it again in silence. His eyes were wide, fixed on Johnny's face.

''The man who killed him,'' Johnny said, ''had taken his room key and cleaned the room out.'' Looking for something? Probably. Almost certainly. It was beginning to form a pattern now. ''But he didn't know about the box in the safe, and he wouldn't have asked you for it even if he had known because he couldn't afford to expose himself, so it stayed right there.'' He paused again. ''Did you take it that next evening, Waldo? As soon as you heard that Wilson had disappeared with his clothing, his luggage?''

There was silence. Johnny got up from the lettuce crate and walked slowly across the room, turned, and came back to stand above Waldo. "Are you married?"

He watched the nod.

"Kids?"

Waldo moistened his lips. "Eight," he said.

It figured, Johnny thought; goddam it, it figured all too well: when poverty and real need touched you, you reacted in your own way. "So you work here days," he said, "and at the motel nights, and it still isn't enough, is it? Never enough for a wife and eight kids and maybe some other relatives too?" He saw the affirmative answer written plain in the man's eyes. "So," Johnny said, "you didn't know what the package was, but you knew it was valuable or Wilson wouldn't have wanted it put in the safe, and Wilson had apparently skipped, so he wasn't going to complain." Another pause. "What was in the box, Waldo?"

"I—" Waldo shook his head, but his eyes clung to Johnny's, pleading.

"You didn't know what it was," Johnny said. "But you probably had a good idea. It was white powder, wasn't it? Wasn't it?"

There was a long pause and then a slow nod.

"So," Johnny said, "you found somebody who did know for sure what it was, and what to do with it. How much did he pay you for it, Waldo?"

The man was beyond resistance now. "Ten dollars. I—thought it was worth more, but I didn't know." He sat slumped, helpless, mute; a born loser.

"And he sold some of it to each of three people," Johnny said. "Probably for a lot more than ten dollars apiece. And they used it. And it killed them." It was not pity that he felt; it was, rather, a cold anger directed against everybody in the chain of circumstances: against Wilson and Wilson's murderer; against Joe Warren who had disposed of Wilson's body; against Waldo and his cupidity and ignorance; but most of all against the last man in the chain. "Who was it, Waldo?"

Waldo closed his eyes. He opened them painfully, close to tears. "My brother-in-law, my own wife's brother."

"So," Johnny said, "he's the one we pick up." He was back at headquarters now, standing at Tony Lopez's desk. "His name is Pete Gardena."

"I know him," Tony said. "He should have been drowned at birth. I know his sister too, Felicia. She's tried to take care of him, keep him out of trouble." Tony shook his head. "Nobody can keep Pete out of trouble."

"When you pick him up," Johnny said, "take him around to see the McDade woman. I want to know if she's seen him going to the porno movies." He shook his head. "It doesn't make sense that he had anything to do with Wilson's death, but we'll check it out anyway."

He walked into his own office and stood for a few moments looking down at his desk. Then, driven by a compulsion against which there was no defense, he turned away and walked out of the building into the fresh air and sunshine.

The plaza was almost empty. Here and there, *turistas* strolled or snapped their cameras or read the inscription on the column commemorating local Indian skirmishes, but none paused to sit. Johnny chose a bench in the sun and plumped himself down on it to let his thoughts go as they would.

Wilson had the bad heroin in his possession. That was the starting point. Where had he come by it, and why was he carrying it? If the narco Snyder's analysis was accurate, and Johnny thought that it was, then Wilson in his role of collector for the organization would normally have carried nothing but money. And why had he wanted the stuff in the motel safe? On the face of it, that rang false. Unless? Silently he asked the one-word question and heard no answer.

Inactivity was suddenly impossible. Johnny stood up and began to walk aimlessly. Unless? There was a word. Fit an answer to it, even a wild guess, and maybe a new direction would reveal itself. All right. Unless Wilson was afraid somebody was going to try to take the heroin away from him—how about that?

Who? And why? Skip the who; concentrate on the why. Okay. Heroin is valuable. But this was bad heroin, poison. Did Wilson know it? Was that why he wanted it locked up? Does that make sense?

Johnny snapped his fingers, and began to walk a little faster. Maybe Wilson knew it was bad heroin, and that was what made it particularly valuable. How about that? Somebody was pushing bad heroin, and Wilson had found out about it? According to Snyder, bad dope, deaths, would be bad for business; that was how the organization would see it. And Wilson was a home office man, no? Was he carrying the bad heroin back to the home office as proof that someone was fouling things up? Or, the converse, was Wilson himself fouling things up by passing bad dope? Think, Juan Felipe; how do you find answers to the questions when the one man who might answer them has been dead for months?

The cathedral bells rang and the pigeons in the towers scattered in frightened, flapping flight. Johnny gazed at the cathedral towers, and thought of a dead man; no, four dead men, Wilson and the three like Martinez who had died from the bad heroin. A new thought was lurking, but it had not yet exposed itself. Why?

The cathedral bells stopped their ringing, and the echoes faded into silence. One pigeon flew back to the tower. Others followed. One pigeon flies, all pigeons fly. One man dies, all men die—from bad heroin. All men? Three men. Are you sure, Juan Felipe? Only three? Only three here in Santo Cristo, but a collector like Wilson would cover a large territory, no? How about other deaths from bad H in other parts of the Southwest? Possible, no?

That, at least, was a direction to look.

Pete Gardena was big, sloppy, and sullen. He sat in Johnny's office and glared at the world. Tony Lopez leaned against the wall. Gardena said, ''Waldo, that little shit, he says I bought dope from him, he's a liar. Where would he get H? He wouldn't know it from nothing.''

''Nobody mentioned H,'' Johnny said.

''So, okay,'' Gardena said. ''What's it supposed to be? Pot?''

''Poison,'' Johnny said. ''It killed three men.'' He named them.

Gardena shook his head wonderingly. "Jesus Christ, you trying to get me for that? You've really flipped. You—"

"Oh, we'll get you," Johnny said. And then, new thought: "Unless somebody else gets you first."

For the first time Gardena's belligerence slipped. "What's that supposed to mean?"

"You bought some dope," Johnny said, "that didn't belong to your brother-in-law." He raised one hand. "You asked a question. I'm answering it. Be quiet." He paused. "You sold three fixes. Three dead men." He paused again. "The people whose dope it was don't like deaths from bad heroin. It's bad for business." A third pause, longer this time. "And they don't like amateurs causing trouble. Amateurs like you. I'd stay out of dark places, if I were you." He stood up. "Turn him loose, Tony. Let's see how far he gets."

Tony tapped Gardena's shoulder. Gardena stood up slowly. He was watching Johnny's face, searching it. "You're having me on."

"Am I?" Johnny shook his head. He was smiling faintly, unpleasantly. "You're the one who knows that. We can't prove anything—yet. And we can't really move until we have proof. But the other people, the ones whose business you've hurt—" He shook his head again, unsmiling this time. "They don't need proof, Gardena. If they're sure, and they probably are, then they may very well decide to make sure you don't get in their way again. They're businessmen, and you're a liability."

Gardena stood irresolute. "You goddam fuzz—" he

began, but the truculence rang false. He swallowed visibly. "Look—"

"Take him away," Johnny said. "He stinks. I'll be in the teletype room." He walked out.

He was standing watching the clacking teletype when Tony came into the room. Tony said, "You scared him but good, amigo."

"That was the idea."

"Did you mean it?"

"I don't know. Wilson had the dope, and I'm guessing he was an organization man." Johnny looked at Tony. "Assuming the guess is correct, what would you think?"

"I would think," Tony said slowly, "that I am glad I am not Pete Gardena."

Johnny nodded. "So would I." He looked at the teletype again. The yellow sheet of paper was rising in short jerks as words became lines and the message clattered on. Johnny read quickly. "And I think we're guessing right," he said. "Look there. Tucson, Phoenix, El Paso—a death from bad H in each, back in December." He looked again at Tony. "While Wilson was still alive." He paused. "It wants looking into, no?"

10

Ben Hart's ranch house was eight miles in on his own dirt road from the cattle guard at the highway. The living room was two-storied, one wall almost entirely of glass facing the great mountains. On this brisk late spring-early summer day a piñon fire burned in the rough stone fireplace. "Always glad to see you, honey," Ben said. "Sit down. Put your feet up. Tell me what's on your mind."

"Now that I'm here," Cassie said, "I don't know how to begin."

"At the beginning," Ben said, "or at the end, or anywhere in between. I'm easy to get along with. Most times." He was smiling.

And there, Cassie thought, was one of the uncertainties. The old man was easy to get along with most times, as he said; but there were other times when he laid back his ears and dug in his heels and refused to budge. Johnny had said it, and Johnny knew: there was no give in the old man, none. "I've been offered a consulting job," Cassie said, "advising, if that's the

96

word, on certain aspects of a new development. Call it applied anthropology.''

Ben heaved himself out of his chair, walked to the fireplace and with the heavy trident fire tool gave one of the logs a savage jab. He leaned the trident gently against the stones and turned back to the room. "Harper?" he said.

Cassie nodded. "And you don't approve."

"I didn't say that, honey." Ben hesitated thoughtfully. "I don't approve of Harper; or let's say I don't particularly cotton to his kind. And I'd rather the land stayed like it is, empty. But hells bells, a lot of things have happened I'd rather hadn't, blacktop roads, fences all over the countryside, too many people, smoke from those goddam power plants two hundred miles away coming down here to mess up what used to be clear air—" Ben spread his hands. "I'm doing what I can to stop Harper even if he doesn't know it yet." He paused. "But if I can't stop him, then I guess I'd rather see somebody like you talking sense to him—if that's possible.''

"I don't know if it is," Cassie said, "but I can try."

Ben was still on his feet, bulky as a bear, and when aroused as dangerous. "Dude from the East," he said. "Represents a lot of money that's looking for a profitable place to roost. They've used up their land back there, people all jammed up like turkeys in a pen. So they want to come out here and use up ours." He shook his head. "Maybe it has to be. I don't know. But over Arizona way, I hear tell, they're selling little teeny lots no more than saddle-blanket size to people back East who've never seen them, who don't know all they're getting is dirt and sage and jackrabbits and horny toads and rattlesnakes with maybe some greasewood and some mesquite thrown in, and water if you can find it but maybe down so deep if at all they couldn't begin to afford to drill the well anyway.''

"I've read about that," Cassie said. "And we don't want it happening here."

Ben sighed. "Maybe you can help keep it from happening, honey," he said. "That is, if I can't light a backfire myself." He waved one hand in a gesture of assent. "Go ahead, take the man's money and make him listen to you."

It was hard to measure the depth of her relief. She was smiling. "Thank you, Ben."

"Now," Ben said, "let's have a drink and talk about something pleasant. I was going to call you anyway. The barbecue's Saturday. Come about noon, you and that Apache of yours." He smiled suddenly. "I won't guarantee when you'll get home."

Johnny was waiting in Cassie's office at the museum. He looked at his watch as she came in. "Little time, chica. The flying machine won't wait." He kissed her briefly. "Tucson, Phoenix, El Paso, in that order. I'll be back—"

"Ben's barbecue is Saturday. You'll be back by then?"

"I wouldn't miss it." He kissed her again, a long kiss this time. Then he held her at arm's length for a moment before he released her. *"Hasta luego, querida."*

"Vayas con Dios." She watched him trot down the

hall toward the front door. She hadn't had a chance to tell him about Harper, she thought; she wondered what he would say when she did.

Johnny sat in the Medical Examiner's office in Tucson and watched the doctor read Doc Easy's carefully detailed autopsy reports. The doctor nodded as he put the papers down. "I'll send you a copy of my report of our death here, lieutenant. It's identical." He studied Johnny's face. "You have an explanation?"

"Maybe." At least the trail had not disappeared. "The man who brought the bad H to Santo Cristo, or at least had it in his possession there, was killed early in January. He might have been through here last December when you had your death." He stood up, collected his papers, tucked them away. "I'll see if I can find out."

"Good luck," the doctor said.

It was not hard, merely tedious. Tucson police cooperated, providing a car and a driver, a large, redheaded, freckled Anglo named Peters who, surprisingly, spoke fluent Spanish. "*Hijo de puta,* son of a whore," he said, "who peddles dope deserves to be strung up by his *cojones.*" Then, in English, "Son of a friend of mine, kid back from Vietnam, he's hooked." He turned in the seat to look directly at Johnny. "Break your goddam heart, and I'd like to break somebody's goddam neck. Where you want to start?"

Johnny had given it thought. "In Santo Cristo," he said, "the man named Wilson stayed at a motel right in the center of town. If we figure him right, he'd want to be handy for contacts, not way out somewhere where he'd be hard to reach.''

"Figures."

"He seems to have made his contacts," Johnny said, "at least some of them, in a porno movie house."

Peters grinned. "How the hell do you tell the difference these days?" They drove off. "Three, four possibilities for motels in town," he said. "We'll just try them out, and see."

It was at motel number five on a quiet side street that they hit pay dirt. "December eighteenth and nineteenth," Peters said, "Walter Wilson, New York City. That your boy?" He handed the registration card to Johnny.

It was unmistakably the same handwriting. Johnny produced his picture of Wilson. The manager shook his head doubtfully. "Maybe, maybe not. That long ago—" He shrugged.

Peters said, "Our boy died the eighteenth." He watched Johnny nod. "Bear down on it," Peters said to the manager.

Johnny said, "Maybe, just maybe he had something to put in the safe?"

The manager was silent for a little time. "What kind of thing? Traveler's checks, money, jewelry?"

Johnny held his hands only a few inches apart. "Maybe a wrapped box about this size." He watched the manager's face brighten. "So?" Johnny said.

The manager nodded. "I remember wondering what it was. It was heavy. But what the hell, it was no business of mine."

Peters was still shuffling through the registration

cards. "Never looked at it before," he said, "but Jesus, they come from all over, don't they?"

"Our climate," the manager said.

Peters was grinning now. "Thought you had pretty fair climate up Santo Cristo way, no?" He waved two cards. "But look here." He handed them to Johnny.

The first card read: Mr. and Mrs. George March, Jr., The Lodge, Santo Cristo. Johnny stared at it. Sonny March and his wife with whom Wilson had dinner at the Lodge.

Peters said, "*Algo*, something?"

"Maybe." Johnny looked at the second card: Paul Harper, Camino Encantado, Santo Cristo. "Maybe a little more than maybe," Johnny said. He jotted down the dates: the Marches had stayed at the motel December 19 and 20; Harper had been there only the night of December 16. "So Harper was gone before Wilson arrived," he said, sitting out in the car again, "but Sonny March and his wife were here while Wilson was." Tony Lopez would have recognized the almost dreamy expression. Then Johnny shook his head. "Maybe nothing," he said. "As far as I know, Harper and Wilson didn't know each other, and the Marches being here could have been pure coincidence."

"Which," Peters said, "you don't believe for a single goddam second, do you?"

The white teeth flashed. "I am a suspicious man, amigo," Johnny said in Spanish.

The next day Phoenix, with the temperature in the nineties, was bursting at the seams with people. Once not too long ago, Johnny thought, here in Arizona even Phoenix had been a sleepy little town dozing in the sun.

And not too long before that, some of his own ancestors had romped through these parts at will, and the
Europeans who lived here, Spanish and Anglos alike,
had ventured out of their towns only in groups, and
then fearfully. The single constant was change, he
thought, and not always for the better.

The Phoenix Medical Examiner checked Doc Easy's
autopsy reports and wasted no time agreeing. "The
only thing different," he said, "is the dates. Our death
was Christmas Day." He paused. "Isn't that a hell of
a day to die?"

As far as Johnny was concerned, one day was as
good, or as bad, as the next, but he nodded solemnly
and went off to check in with the Phoenix police.

The routine was as in Tucson, except that the patrol
car driver was named Gonzalez. "In the center of
town?" Gonzalez said. "Maybe. We'll try, anyway."
His sideways glance was covertly resentful. "This isn't
a border town. We're civilized here."

Johnny said nothing.

"What I mean," Gonzalez said, "is that we're rough
on pushers. Law and order, you know what I mean?
You're looking for an organization, you come to the
wrong place. Try Vegas or LA."

"But as long as I'm here," Johnny said, "I'll try
here, okay?"

"Okay!" Gonzalez wrenched the car around in a
U turn. "I do what I'm told."

It took six stops this time. Johnny looked at the card
in his hand. "Walter Wilson, New York City, December twenty-first through December twenty-fifth." He
held out the picture to the manager. Gonzalez glared.

The manager said, "I recognize him. Whether the name Wilson fits him—" He shrugged.

"Couple of things about him," Johnny said. "He had a little wrapped box so big, and he probably wanted it in your safe." He saw no sign of recollection in the manager's face. "And," Johnny said, "he drank Dubonnet and tonic."

The manager began to smile. "I remember him now. Never heard of Dubonnet and tonic before. The barman told me. Now I remember the little box, too." He nodded. "The name Wilson fits."

Gonzalez scowled and said nothing. Johnny was riffling through the other December cards. No Marches. But there was Paul Harper again, December 17, the night after Tucson, and what, if anything, did that mean? But he wrote it all down.

Out in the car again, Gonzalez said, "What about the little box? What makes it important?" The resentment in his tone was open now.

"Your civic pride's hanging out," Johnny said. In a way it was amusing. "What was left in the little box by the time he got to Santo Cristo was enough bad H to kill three men." And he could not resist adding, "Maybe you're rough on the wrong people in your law-and-order way."

He flew off the next day to El Paso where, it amused him to remember, the Spanish from Santo Cristo had finally stopped running in 1680 after the Pueblo revolt. More change, Johnny thought, but also found himself wondering if their bags and hang-ups back then were really much different from those of today. Seventeenth-century cops, whatever they were called, probably dealt most of the time, just as he did, with theft and crimes of violence, so maybe man, who liked to think he had progressed, was really just moving in circles. My thought for the day, Johnny told himself, and went off to find the Medical Examiner.

This one was talkative. "The same autopsy reports, no doubt about it." He looked hard at Johnny. "You say Tucson and Phoenix as well? How do you account for that, lieutenant?"

"I'm trying," Johnny said.

"It isn't like somebody going down from an overdose," the doctor said. "That happens. The drug can kill even if it's pure. Hell, as far as that goes, aspirin can kill. But we're talking here about poisoned heroin, and that has to be deliberate. Why?"

"All I have is a couple of ideas," Johnny said.

The doctor studied him. "And you aren't about to babble them around until you know more." He nodded. "Good thinking, lieutenant. I wish more people would keep their mouths shut until they know what they're talking about. Politicians aside, even some blabbermouths in my own profession—never mind. If I can help you, let me know. I hope there is a special hot corner of hell reserved for dope peddlers, even if what they sell isn't poisoned."

Johnny flew back to Santo Cristo and drove to Cassie's house on Arroyo Road in time for dinner Friday evening. Chico capered and laughed in his joy, and Cassie, smiling, walked into Johnny's arms and pressed herself close against him. "We missed you."

"Did you now?" Johnny took out a small, flat, paper

package and put it in her hand. "Found this in Tucson." He was shy as a boy as he watched her unwrap the paper.

"Johnny, it's lovely!" A fine slice through a geode, the thin outer crust encased in silver, the whole attached to a silver chain. The tiny crystals in the center of the geode glistened in shades of yellow and tan. Cassie hung it around her neck. The crystalline slice hung between her breasts. "Lovely," she said again.

And Johnny, smiling, said, "I agree."

They sat with drinks after dinner in front of the fire. Johnny talked of Wilson in Tucson, Phoenix, and El Paso. "The motel where he stayed in El Paso is near the airport. It could mean that he made contacts there from out of town." He looked at his notebook. "He was there the twenty-sixth through New Year's Eve. He came here New Year's Day. No record of the Marches in El Paso, but Paul Harper was there December twenty-fourth. The El Paso death was December twenty-sixth." He sat in silence for a few moments, staring at the notebook page. "Funny," he said.

"Johnny." Cassie's voice was quiet, grave. "What does Paul Harper have to do with it?"

"I don't know, chica. But when coincidences stick out like these, you wonder." His attention was still on the notebook page. "Wilson knew the Marches. He had dinner with them here in Santo Cristo one of the two or three days before he was killed."

"Maybe he just happened to meet them in Tucson." Cassie's smooth café-au-lait face was expressionless. "And they told him to look them up when he got to Santo Cristo."

"Possible," Johnny said. "But Harper is a horse of another color."

"Tell me why."

Johnny looked at her carefully. "Chica, you can see it yourself."

"Tell me anyway."

There was something between them, and Johnny did not know what. He nodded slowly. "Okay. At each stop, Harper has preceded Wilson at the same motel by only a matter of a few days. One day in Tucson, four days in Phoenix, two days in El Paso."

"And what does that mean?"

"They're not even the same motel chain," Johnny said. "It would be different if they were all, say Holiday Inns. Then you'd make reservations from one to the other. But these are all different motels in different cities, yet where Wilson stayed, Harper had been there first. Doesn't that strike you as odd?"

"They didn't meet."

"No, chica, they didn't meet as far as I know. But there's one more thing. Two of the deaths, Tucson and El Paso, occurred the day Wilson arrived. But Harper had been in each city at least two days before each death."

"Johnny."

Johnny closed the notebook with careful deliberation. "What's bugging you?"

"What you're implying. With no proof. None. It—it isn't like you." It was very much like him to explore a hunch, but at the moment she would not for the world have admitted it.

"I'm guessing, chica," Johnny said. "I admit it. All I've said is that it looks funny. Wilson had a little box, presumably the same one that ended in Pete Gardena's hands here, all the way from Tucson to Phoenix to El Paso. At each stop he had it put in the motel safe. I'm guessing that that was because he handled money instead of dope and he didn't even like to carry the box, but he felt he had to."

"Why? Why not put it in the mail to his home office you've dreamed up?"

"Don't get belligerent with me, chica." His voice was quiet, too quiet. He waited, but there was no answer. "If I'm right," Johnny said, "he wouldn't have trusted the mail because he wouldn't know who would open the package at the other end. If he, Wilson, had found a foul-up in the organization, then he wouldn't know how many or who might be involved. So he would carry the package and turn it over personally."

Cassie said slowly, carefully, "How can you be sure there was a foul-up that he had found?"

"Three men died from poisoned dope, one of them the day he arrived in Tucson." He paused. "Two days after Harper had been there."

"There you go again," Cassie said. "You're implying that Paul Harper had something to do with it, and that's ridiculous."

"Maybe." Johnny stared at the fire for a long time in silence. Chico got up from the floor and thrust his cold nose into Johnny's hand. Johnny squeezed his muzzle gently. He said at last, "I don't know what's going on, chica—"

"Nothing is going on."

"Okay," Johnny said, "we'll say that nothing is going on. Here are my reasons for wondering about Harper." He held up his hand and ticked off the points as he spoke. "We know that Wilson had poisoned dope, carried a gun, and probably wore a money belt. We tie him to an organization, probably as a collector. I find him staying at particular motels in three different cities. Now Wilson's contacts would want to know where to reach him. So I am guessing that those particular motels had been designated as *the* places to stay, probably not each time Wilson came through, but on this particular trip."

"Pure guesswork," Cassie said.

"Agreed. But it hangs together. And if it is right, then it's too much of a coincidence that Harper stayed at each of those designated motels out of the hundred or so in those three cities, only days before Wilson arrived." He paused. "And only days before a man died of poisoned dope in each city."

The geode slice between her breasts was unsteady with Cassie's breathing. "Johnny, listen to me. Paul is a businessman. He is investing millions in the land he is developing. Does it make sense of any kind that he would be mixed up with a dope ring?"

"Paul," Johnny said.

"I'm doing consulting work for him."

"*Verdad?*" Johnny's face showed nothing. "I didn't think you liked him much."

"I've changed my mind. He's a nice man, intelligent, well-educated, generous, considerate—" Cassie shook her head angrily. "Clichés, silly, corny cliché-words, but they're true."

Johnny nodded. He stood up slowly. "An' me," he said in singsong, "I'm estupid Indian cop weeth no more sense than to theenk maybe he ees not all that he seem to be." He paused. "Sorry about that, chica." The fake accent was gone.

"Sit down, Johnny."

He remained standing, looking down at her, waiting, expressionless.

"I said I was doing consulting work for him," Cassie said. "That is all. I know something of his background and his references in the East, and it is inconceivable to me that he could be mixed up in any kind of—" She stopped and shook her head. "Please let's not fight."

Johnny turned away and walked slowly across the room. He stood for a few moments facing the wall, and then turned and walked back to stand as before looking down at her. "Chica," he said, "we're going to butt heads over Harper whether I want to or not until I find out whether my guesswork is right or wrong. There are seven dead men and somebody is responsible." He paused. "And I'm a cop."

Cassie closed her eyes. When she opened them they were filled with tears. She stood up from the sofa. "Oh, God, Johnny, don't let it—spoil us!"

Johnny put his arms around her and she came to him willingly. He held her tight. "Chica. Chica." He stroked her head. He had no words, only thoughts: I don't like your guts, Harper, whatever you are, and if I have to I'll cut them out with a dull knife and stuff them down your throat. Aloud he said, "It's late, chica, and it's been a long day." He lifted her chin with his hand and smiled down at her. "And tomorrow's going to be another, or I don't know Ben Hart."

Cassie nodded. Her smile was unsteady. "Let's go to bed. Sometimes that's the best solution for everything." The smile spread. "Thus speaks the anthropologist."

11

Ben Hart's barbecue will not go down in history, but all agreed that it was a good solid bash.

Both senators flew in from Washington. Old Ben Hart deserved as much, and, besides, a little political fence-riding never did anyone harm.

Mark Hawley of course was there.

The state's other congressman wasn't even invited. He represented the other, southern half of the state, which was bad enough, but his daddy and Ben had once tangled in public, leaving the congressman's daddy to be carried away for extensive repairs, and relations had been a trifle strained ever since. Besides, the other congressman was a renowned and vocal teetotaler, and that in itself would have been sufficient to bar him from the guest list.

The governor came, and the lieutenant governor. They were not on speaking terms, and from time to time during the afternoon and evening they were to be seen walking around each other warily in the manner of strange dogs passing in a narrow lane.

"We have a built-in adversary system of government," Mark Hawley pointed out to Cassie, "but it does have its benefits. In most states the governor is free to gallivant around making speeches and trying to get on national television. But Joe is afraid to leave the state because soon as he does by law Pete takes over, and Joe isn't sure he'd even be allowed back in. So he stays home and, having nothing better to do, attends to business."

There were ranchers with wives and some children. If they came from nearby, they drove; some of the more distant ones flew their own planes and landed in the open field beyond the row of windbreak poplars.

The Board of County Supervisors was there en masse, three of them constantly apprehensive that Ben Hart's inevitable arm-twisting against the proposed land development might dislocate a shoulder joint. The remaining three wore smug expressions and enjoyed themselves mightily on barbecued beef, venison, and *cabrito;* accompanied by ranch style beans, Indian bread baked in beehive-shaped adobe ovens, corn on the cob flown in from a warmer climate; followed by home-baked pies; the whole washed down with beer, whiskey, or coffee, milk for the young ones—food that would, and did, stick to a man's backbone and cause a woman to worry about her weight.

The talk, and there was a great deal of it, was in English, Spanish, and the local *mezcla*, or blend.

The day was fair, clear, bright, and without wind. On the mountains above the 11,000-foot timber-line, snow still clung, and although it was too far away to see, you knew that the tiny, hardy Alpine plants were pushing their way into sunshine.

Two turkey vultures, attracted by the commotion and the possibility of leavings, circled for a time high above, rocking on their dihedral wings, and, presumably, watching events with interest. A single red-tailed hawk soared past effortlessly riding the thermals. On the horizon, one hundred air miles away, Mount Taylor showed plain and clear.

The two senators and Mark Hawley sat with Ben on wooden benches at a trestle table, drinks at hand. The talk was quiet, filled with reminiscences and seemingly without point, although Mark Hawley summed it all up with: "So what it amounts to is we don't really want carpetbaggers moving in, slicing up the country-side and selling it piecemeal all over the East." No one challenged the point. "On the other hand," Hawley said, "no one of us is going to be damn fool enough to come out foursquare against progress and prosperity and as much of that Eastern mattress money as a man can honestly get his hands on." He looked around the table.

The senior senator said, "I think that is a fair assessment."

Ben Hart sighed without rancor. "Does anybody know the Indian word for forked-tongue?" He got up from the bench. "It's no wonder we have a bad name for treaties. Enjoy yourselves." He rolled off to see how the whiskey and beer were holding out.

Doc Easy, carrying tin plate and heavy mug filled with whiskey, spotted Johnny and Cassie and moved toward them. He seemed glum. "Reason," he said, "is

I've got to go East tomorrow, and when I step off the plane at Logan Airport into that flatland humidity I know I'll think I'm breathing under water.'' He had an appreciative pull at the mug. ''My brother,'' he said. ''He's nine years younger than I am, and if he lasts another winter I'll miss my guess. I came out here six years ago figuring I didn't have long. Now—'' He shook his head at the wonder of still being alive and useful.

Cassie, smiling, said, ''John Gore over there came out here to die. That was thirty years ago. He walked up to the top of Cloud Mesa last fall to see our dig. He wasn't even breathing hard.''

Johnny said, ''You take care of her for a few minutes, Doc. I don't want anybody sneaking up and dragging her away.'' He walked off.

Doc, watching Johnny's back, said, ''What's bothering him?''

Cassie shook her head. She was smiling no longer.

Mark Hawley and the two senators had left the trestle table and scattered for convivial purposes. Johnny caught up with Hawley. ''I'd like a favor.''

''Within reason, son.''

Johnny was direct, even brusque. ''Do you have any influence with the Treasury Department?''

''Why,'' the congressman said, ''I've had occasion over the years to twist a few Treasury arms. And one of my committees sometimes tells them how they ought to behave.'' He paused and studied Johnny's face. ''You're uptight, son. What's the problem? Income tax?''

''No.''

The congressman looked around. The nearest trestle

table was empty. "Let's sit," he said. "You look like a man with something on his mind."

"I am," Johnny said. And when they were seated, "Six men dead from poisoned heroin," he said, "and one man dead from a sharp point of something shoved into his spinal cord." He paused.

The congressman nodded. "Heroin," he said, "Treasury, narcotics bureau." He nodded again. "Go on, son."

"I'm going way out," Johnny said.

Hawley sipped his whiskey unperturbed. "Fire away."

Johnny explained about the motel registration cards in Tucson, Phoenix, and El Paso; at the first motel the Sonny Marches, Harper, and Wilson; at the other two only Wilson and Harper from Santo Cristo. He explained about the small box kept in motel safes, about the hideaway holster Wilson wore, and the missing belt. He had lain awake late last night, Cassie asleep at his side, staring up into the darkness, putting thoughts together, and liking them not.

Hawley said, "You've got a lot of pieces, son. Think you can put them into a pattern?"

"I don't know." The flat-topped bulk of Cloud Mesa dominated the nearby landscape. Johnny stared at it thoughtfully. "Organization money," he said. "I read that it's invested in a lot of things, hotels and casinos in Nevada, in Miami, maybe Puerto Rico, loan businesses all over the place—" He stopped and turned to look at Hawley.

Hawley nodded. "Not much doubt." He held his whiskey unnoticed now. "Go on."

"Twenty-five sections," Johnny said, "sixteen thousand acres for development. Three hundred dollars an acre, I heard. That's four million eight hundred thousand dollars."

"Somewhat more than walking-around money," the congressman said. He set the whiskey glass down and leaned back, clasping one knee with both hands. "Link it up, son."

"Harper," Johnny said.

"I kind of figured that was it." The congressman's voice was mild. "You don't like him, do you?"

"I don't like him," Johnny said. "But I don't like coincidences, either." He explained his reasoning that put Harper at three widely separated motels at which Wilson also stayed only a few days later. "I can't swallow that as chance. If Wilson worked for an organization, and it seems obvious that he did, then Harper has some connection too or he wouldn't have hit those three motels. And Harper is the man handling the land development—"

"So just maybe," the congressman said, "it's organization money behind him, the way you see it?"

"Does it make sense?"

The congressman thought about it. "Maybe." He paused. "What do you want from me?"

"Two things," Johnny said. "If you can get the Treasury people interested, then maybe they can find out who is really behind Harper with all that money, and if there is any suspicion that the money isn't legitimate."

Hawley sat up, picked up his glass and studied it for a few moments in silence. "What's the other thing?"

"There's a Treasury narco named Snyder. He's based in Dallas. We get along. Can we have him here in Santo Cristo for a little while?"

"Working for you?"

Johnny shook his head. "With me, us. We have the local knowledge and some ideas. But he can see farther than we can and he can move around."

"Tucson, Phoenix, El Paso?"

"For a start. Wilson may have covered a lot of other towns, and probably did. Tucson, Phoenix, and El Paso only stand out because poisoned H turned up in each of them and a man died."

The congressman sipped his whiskey thoughtfully. He set the glass down and nodded. "I'll see what I can do, son." He looked beyond Johnny and saw Cassie walking purposefully toward them. "I'll let you know," he said, and stood up. "Join us, honey," he said. "My drink's dry and you and Johnny don't have any. Let's do something about that."

Over by the paddock fence, Ben Hart had one of the county supervisors cornered. "Ever been East, son?"

The supervisor shook his head.

"You've been over to Albuquerque, Dallas, Phoenix, maybe LA?"

"Yes, I mean, sure. I was born in Albuquerque."

Ben nodded. "Thirty, forty years ago it was a nice little town, wasn't it? Sort of a wide place on sixty-six. Like to live there now?"

"The trouble," the supervisor said, trying to evade the question and come to the point, "is that we don't have the authority to say what can be done and what can't. Most people don't understand that. We don't have zoning. We don't—''

''You have water control, don't you? It's been a long time since a man could just drill a well wherever he wanted without asking some kind of permission.''

''Mr. Harper's hydrologist has made a thorough study and he says there is ample water.''

''Hydrologists,'' Ben said, ''are like head-shrinkers, or like what old Teddy Roosevelt used to say about Harvard College men: you can find one on both sides of every damn fool question.'' He paused. ''Point is, son, you know and I know that there isn't enough water for twenty thousand people on that land, no matter what a tame hydrologist says. Maybe some day they'll get de-salting down where people can afford it, and maybe then they'll pipe de-salted water up from the Gulf the way they pipe oil and gas now, but that sure as hell isn't going to happen next Tuesday, and in the meantime a lot of people are going to be awful dry looking for water that isn't where one hydrologist says it is and another says it isn't. You go out to LA and ask there. Spring Street, right smack dab in the middle of the city used to be just that—a place where spring water ran. There used to be artesian wells, flowing wells, all the way out to San Berdoo. All you had to do was drill and the water came up at you. They used that up. Then they built a pipeline up to Owens Valley, as nice and green a little valley as ever you did see. They sucked it dry. It's a desert now. They've reached down to the Colorado River for water, and that isn't the end. God only knows where the end is. And right here we start with what is damn near desert to begin with.'' The old man seemed to swell. He poked the supervisor's shoulder with a forefinger stiff as a drill rod. "If you don't have the authority to say what can and what can't be done," Ben said, "then you'd goddam well better get it before this country is ruined and some folks come looking for those who let it be done." He paused. "With horsewhips, mister, at the very least." He paused again. "Now go get a drink and enjoy yourself."

Mark Hawley found Ben and led him into a backwater of quiet. "Sonny and Betty March," the congressman said, "they on your list?"

Ben nodded. "I left an invitation at the Lodge. If they're back from the Caribbean, I expect they'll come along." He studied the congressman's face. "Why?"

"I want to talk to Sonny about a fellow." He saw the question forming in Ben's face, and promptly forestalled it. "Now don't get nosy. It may have nothing to do with you, probably doesn't." But the temptation to needle was too strong to resist. "On the other hand," the congressman said, "you just may have people working on your side you don't even know about. Do you see what I mean?"

"No," said Ben.

The congressman nodded contentedly. "A little confusion always makes things interesting. I think I'll sample a bit more of your whiskey. It isn't bad."

Sonny and Betty March did arrive in Sonny's new twelve-cylinder Jaguar trailing a plume of dust the eight miles from the highway. "Just flew in this morning," Betty told Ben, "and found your darling invitation and we wouldn't have missed it for the world. We haven't even unpacked, and I don't think we will because there's a man named Ross in the cottage we always have, and he simply refuses to move and for some reason Sonny won't push Sam Christopher the manager even the slightest bit—'' She had to pause for breath.

"It's only for a day or two," Sonny said. "Now let's forget it." He looked around, wearing his party smile. "All these people we haven't seen for months." Sonny was tall and tanned and fit, well-tailored and well-groomed, in his early forties. "It's good to be back, Ben," he said.

"Find something to carry with you," Ben said, "and make yourselves at home." He watched them move toward the bar, and he saw Mark Hawley set an intersecting course.

The congressman caught them without seeming to. "Sonny," he said, "Betty, welcome back." He stepped aside. "Get drinks in your hands." He paused. "And then, son, I'd like a word with you."

Away from the press, at one of the empty trestle tables, "Just back?" the congressman said to Sonny, and nodded. "Then you won't have caught up yet on local news."

Sonny smiled. "Eager to hear. Who is divorced or is sleeping with whom?"

"A little different," the congressman said. He studied his whiskey. "They found a dead man up on the ski slope, and that kind of overshadowed the social page." He looked at Sonny then, his face entirely guileless. "And of course there's the new development on the old Raven land. Eastern money. And, oh, yes, Newton Berry's shop was bombed, how about that?" He took a sip of his whiskey and sighed in contentment. "Dead man's name," he said, "was Wilson, Walter Wilson." He was watching Sonny's eyes.

They changed, although the congressman had to admit that the change was faint, almost imperceptible. He had not realized that Sonny was capable of such careful control.

"Walter Wilson," Sonny said, and added no more.

"Mystery man," the congressman said. "Nobody seems to know anything about him." He smiled, dismissing the subject. "What I wanted to talk to you about was the Caribbean in general and Haiti in particular. Always like to keep up on fresh reactions to places where our foreign aid goes."

Sonny smiled. "Whatever I can tell you," he said.

The congressman wondered. It was possible, he was beginning to think, that there was more to Sonny March than met the eye.

12

He was a pleasant man, this Paul Harper, Cassie had found. He didn't push, and he listened quietly and with respect to her opinions, and although he hadn't made any kind of pass at her yet, what showed at times in his eyes did her female ego no harm at all. Cassie did not think of herself as a sex symbol, liberated or not; on the other hand, the body she had been born with and had developed was, as she well knew, a thing of slim, rounded beauty, and as long as the sex urge did exist, and what anthropologist could deny it, she saw nothing demeaning in absorbing whatever admiration and even advantage happened to be handy.

She sat now in Harper's development office just off the plaza. "The basic fact as I see it," she said, "is that you are planning to add fifty per cent to the population of Santo Cristo. That means half again as much of everything is going to be needed—water, of course, but also electricity and gas and sewage disposal, schools, hospital space, police and fire protection, all of the goods and services people demand—and jobs."

Cassie paused. "What are these people going to do to earn their living?"

Harper nodded. "You have a point." His voice was quiet, polite. "But that isn't really our responsibility, is it?" He had an easy smile. "When someone buys property, I don't think he expects to find a guaranteed job written into the title. You are seeing deep, as I hoped you would. But perhaps you are seeing a little too deep?"

Maybe, Cassie thought; maybe not. "The word ecology has taken on strange meanings these days," she said. "But basically what it means is the relationship between an organism and its environment. If that relationship is in balance, fine. If it isn't, you have problems." She paused. "Am I laboring the obvious?"

"Not at all." Harper was smiling, and there was that look in his eye, that flattering man-to-attractive-woman look, hard to resist: "I'm interested," Harper said.

In what she was saying, or in her? "Well," Cassie said, "let's take an example. My dig shows that a number of people, perhaps as many as five hundred, lived for maybe a century, maybe longer, on top of Cloud Mesa. They raised their crops down on the flat; they carried what water they needed for domestic use up the path in earthenware pots they had made for themselves. They hunted. Their lives were apparently not overly burdensome, and their position seemed to be secure. Their relationship with their environment was in balance." Cassie paused. "Then they left the mesa. Quite suddenly. And we don't know why." She paused again. "But we can be pretty sure of one generalization. Whatever it was that caused them to leave was something that destroyed the balance of their relationship with their environment. It may have been drought that made crop-raising impossible or at least insufficient for their needs. It may have been a lack of game to hunt. It may have been that enemies drove them away. It may even have been, as some think, that they felt that somehow their gods had become displeased, and movement to a new location was the only satisfactory solution." One more pause. "But the point is that the balance between those people and their mesa-top environment had been destroyed, and something had to be done."

Harper, smiling still, said, "Bring it closer to home."

Cassie nodded. "Forty thousand people live here in Santo Cristo. There is water enough for them, land enough for them, jobs to support them. But there is no industry here that could suddenly expand to provide employment for a whole new labor force, and that is exactly what you are planning to bring into the area. So the balance could be badly upset." She shook her head. "I'm not earning what you pay me, Paul. All I do is drag my feet."

"I have no complaints." Easy, calm, generous.

And this, Cassie thought, was the man Johnny had set his sights on. She found it hard to believe that Johnny could be so wrong, and in the end, she was confident, he would see his error in suspecting Harper of heaven only knew what lengths of rascality; but in the meantime matters were going to become more unpleasant before they changed for the better. She had seen Johnny on a trail before, or what he was convinced was a trail; and the sight was chilling. There was about him an implacability that matched nothing Cassie had ever seen before. Then, a strange, new, unnerving thought: to what lengths could that implacability lead him? To a conviction that he had the right man even when he was wrong?

"You've drifted away from me, Cassie," Harper said. "Which way are your thoughts running now?"

"In circles." Not true; they were running very much on a straight line—Tucson to Phoenix to El Paso, motel to motel to motel where Walter Wilson had followed. Why? She said, "How did you come to pick Santo Cristo in the first place?"

Harper leaned back in his chair. His smile was untouched. "Easy. I looked at other places first where the climate was at least possible."

"Tucson?" Cassie said.

"One of the first."

"Phoenix? El Paso?" Was she being subtle? Spoken aloud the names did not sound subtle at all. But Harper was unperturbed.

"All of them," he said, "and two or three others. But land was available here at a reasonable price, and development hasn't moved in here as it has in those other places." His smile spread suddenly. "So the relationship with the environment isn't yet out of balance." He paused. "Funny," he said, "that you should have hit on those three places—Tucson, Phoenix, El Paso. I was down there last December, in each city. With time out for a quick jump down to Mexico City between Phoenix and El Paso. Do you know Mexico City, Cassie?"

Cassie nodded. She knew it well.

"A fellow I wanted to see," Harper said. "One of those types who's always on the move." He glanced at his watch and sat up straight. "I didn't think my stomach was lying. How about a drink and some lunch?"

"I should go back to the museum," Cassie said. Nonsense. There was nothing that required her attention.

"If there is one thing I enjoy more than a lot of others," Harper said, "it is walking into a good restaurant with time on my hands and a pretty woman on my arm." He stood up. "Call it business. I want to hear more about the environment."

"I told you I'm not earning my pay."

"All the more reason to have lunch with me and teach me more."

Sonny March parked the twelve-cylinder Jag on Santiago Street where it crouched among lesser automobiles like a cheetah among rabbits. Sonny strolled around the plaza enjoying the sunshine and the clear air and the sight of a mini-skirted *turista,* round haunches waggling as she hurried from spot to spot with her Instamatic camera.

Sonny was in no hurry. He rarely was. Life for Sonny was a long succession of leisurely moves from pleasure to pleasure or place to place. Hurry was for other, less fortunate people. Sometimes Betty tended to rush, and her haste was vaguely annoying. Sometimes Betty tended to push, too, as in that matter of getting Peter Ross and family out of the cottage Sonny and Betty always took at the Lodge. But Sonny could play well the role of immovable object, and that was that. Sonny had absolutely no intention of going up against Peter Ross in anything any place any time; no way. If Betty had asked him why, he wouldn't have told her; but even if he had, she would have thought he was making it up, and he wasn't.

He turned off the plaza and walked up to the alley where the BITS AND PIECES sign hung. As usual the place reeked of incense. Newton Berry came out of his little office in answer to the hanging door bell.

"Mr. March." The words and the tone were polite, but somehow distant. Berry did not offer to shake hands.

Sonny looked around. The shop appeared the same as ever; perhaps fewer items than he remembered, but, then, stock would inevitably fluctuate between Berry's buying trips. "I heard you had a little trouble," Sonny said.

"It was terrible, terrible." Berry's hands moved quickly. "I can't imagine why anyone would do such a horrible thing. The volunteer fireman said that the bomb was dropped, simply dropped right down the chimney." He pointed to the corner fireplace.

"And," Sonny said, "you can't imagine why." It was an uninflected statement, but it seemed to hang, shimmering like a blunt question asked.

Berry said, "Ah, did you have a pleasant winter?"

"Very. Thanks." Sonny smiled. He walked across the shop to a rug that caught his eye, fingered its strong texture. "Nice."

"It isn't for sale, Mr. March. That is, it's already sold."

Sonny turned slowly. "You wouldn't be putting me on, would you?"

"To a man named Ross," Berry said almost desperately. "He and his wife and daughter are staying at the Lodge. Mr. Ross asked me to send the rug to his home. In Westchester." He was watching Sonny's face. "Have I said something wrong?"

"No," Sonny said. "Nothing at all." He walked to a table and picked up a large oval brooch, stood looking down at it unseeing.

"Burmese amber," Berry said. "A very fine example of pierced work. It would go beautifully with Mrs. March's lovely complexion. And the price is quite reasonable."

Sonny put the brooch down. "I was thinking rather the other way around," he said. "I brought something to sell you."

The reaction was immediate and unmistakable: fright. "No!" Berry's voice had risen a full octave. "I don't want to be unreasonable, Mr. March, but no. I— simply can't afford to buy anything. It would be a mistake, a terrible mistake. Please understand. I don't want to offend anyone. I'm a peaceable man and I can't stand unpleasantness. It upsets me. Terribly. Please understand."

Sonny stood for a little time in silence. Slowly he nodded. "I think I do," he said. "I think I understand very well." He was studying Berry closely.

"Please," Berry said. "I am not a talkative man, either, Mr. March. I keep my own counsel. I have no— intimates with whom I gossip, and as far as the police are concerned—"

Sonny said quickly, "Police?"

"Of course they had to—investigate the bombing." Berry's hands moved quickly again, in supplication this time. "You understand. You must understand. They simply terrified me. That one, his face reminds me of those horrible carvings in Mexico, you can almost see him with his obsidian knife simply tearing the living heart from a human sacrifice. I tell you, Mr. March—"

"The question," Sonny said, "is what did you tell them?"

"Nothing. Absolutely nothing. I told them I simply could not imagine why anyone should be so beastly as to drop a bomb among my poor *cosas*, my things." Berry took a deep breath. "You must believe that, Mr. March."

Sonny thought about it. Slowly he nodded. "I guess I'd better," he said.

He walked out of the shop into the bright sunshine, turned down to the plaza, and walked across it. The mini-skirted *turista* was still prancing about snapping her Instamatic. She was braless and her not inconsiderable breasts bounced appealingly. Sonny did not even notice.

He crossed the street to the hotel and walked into its cool dimness. During fiesta its restrooms were closed to the public, but now they were open. Sonny put a dime in the lock of one of the cubicles, went inside, and carefully locked the door behind him. Then from beneath his shirt he drew out a flat nylon bag, opened one end, and began to pour white powder into the toilet bowl. It took four flushings of the toilet before all of the white powder was gone. Sonny flushed the bag down the toilet too and sighed as he unlocked the door.

It was not the money involved, he told himself. He could well afford the loss. But the taste of failure was unpleasant; it irked him that prudence demanded that he give up what had been, after all, lucrative fun, a game of wits on which he had turned a pleasing profit, as with the turn of a card or the spin of the wheel in Las Vegas or Monaco. That was what rankled. But, he told himself as he walked back out into the sunshine, there were times when only a fool failed to cash in his chips and get out of the game. Peter Ross *and* that cop Berry had so luridly described. No way.

By the time he started across the plaza again he was feeling better. This time he noticed that the *turista* looked quite as appealing from the front as from the rear. He sat down on a nearby bench to admire the view.

13

Snyder, the Treasury narcotics agent flown in from Dallas, said, "When your Congressman Hawley says, 'frog,' the Treasury doesn't exactly jump, but it does listen." He was smiling, not displeased with this new assignment. "When they stay in Congress as long as he has, they carry weight. Now bring me up to date."

Johnny brought him up to date.

Snyder thought about it and nodded slowly. "I think you have Wilson tabbed right. And that would seem to link Harper in some way. Too much coincidence otherwise." He was silent for a little time. "The heroin was poisoned? It wasn't just impure?"

"Poisoned," Johnny said. "And whoever did it meant business. Cyanide."

"Why poison it?"

"I've thought about that," Johnny said, "and it seems to me that it almost had to be done to discredit somebody."

Snyder smiled. "You're kidding. Six people dead from it, and you think it was done just to make somebody look bad.'' He shook his head, smiling still. ''Come on.''

A year ago, before Cassie, Johnny thought, he would have tightened up in the face of mockery. He didn't like it much now, but it didn't really touch him. ''Three of those deaths, remember,'' he said, ''were accidental. The heroin ought to have been on its way to the home office, not in the hands of a punk named Pete Gardena who didn't know what he was doing, and wouldn't have cared if he had. He would sell his mother for a short beer.''

Snyder's smile began to fade. ''I'd forgotten that. Still.''

''The other three deaths,'' Johnny said, ''were widely spaced, different cities, presumably different pushers. One death in each place to make a point?'' He paused to give Snyder time to think about it. ''You said it yourself,'' Johnny said. ''Maybe somebody is trying to move in, take over by making the organization look bad. Suppose the pushers can't trust the dope they get from the organization distributor because every now and again it kills a customer? And a new source turns up with good H? What then?''

Snyder tugged at an ear lobe. ''I see what you mean. It could be.''

''I'm not saying that's how it was,'' Johnny said, ''but it's a possibility that fits. Somebody went to some trouble to poison at least enough for six fixes. Wilson on his collection trip found out about it and somehow got his hands on some of it.''

''Maybe Wilson was passing it himself.''

Johnny nodded. ''It could be, but I doubt it. We've

set Wilson as a collector, not a distributor, although there'd be nothing to prevent him from using his contacts." He paused thoughtfully. "Once," he said, "He'd be a damn fool to try it a second time, and even once would make him stand out in everybody's memory because he'd have stepped out of his role." He paused again. "But the other thing is that two of the deaths, Tucson and El Paso, occurred the day Wilson arrived in town, and that's a little too fast, and a little too obvious. I should think whoever passed the bad dope would want to be out of town before anybody turned up dead."

Snyder leaned back in his chair and studied Johnny's face. "You have this fellow Harper in mind? What kind of man is he?"

"I've never met him." It was hard to think of Cassie's description without pain. "I'm told he's a nice fellow, intelligent, well-educated, generous, and considerate." Johnny spoke the words without inflection.

"And," Snyder said, "he's probably good to his mother and likes dogs and children and helps old ladies across the street, is that it?"

"That," Johnny said, "is about it. He has a lot of Eastern money behind him and maybe some of it is even his own. I don't know a thing against him except that he stayed in those three motels and a few days after he left each town somebody died from bad dope." And, he thought, my girl calls him by his first name and stands up to defend him, so I'm trying to lean over backward when I talk about the bastard.

Snyder sighed and stood up. "I'll be in touch."

Johnny sat for a time after Snyder was gone, just

staring at the wall. Once upon a time, he thought, by which he meant in that wasteland he lived in before Cassie, he had never had any trouble with emotions creeping in to distort judgment, because he had looked at everybody alike, or near enough. Now, he told himself, because of Cassie he was seeing Harper around every corner and under every bed, and that was purely no way to conduct an investigation. There were other possibilities, dangling threads, and he had damn well better run them down too. He went out to his pick-up and drove the eight miles to the Lodge.

Sam Christopher was behind the desk and preoccupied with room arrangements for a party of six Texanos who would be flying in tomorrow. He heard Johnny's question and answered automatically: "Cottage A. The Marches always have Cottage A." He did not look up as Johnny walked straight through the lobby without using the house phone.

And so Johnny met Peter Ross, a meeting without reason. "They told me at the desk that the Marches were in Cottage A," Johnny said.

"They made a mistake. My name is Ross." Ross was quiet, polite.

"It was Sam Christopher," Johnny said. "He said the Marches always have Cottage A."

"I don't even know the Marches." Still quiet, still polite, but with a trace of impatience showing now.

From inside the cottage a girl's voice said, "Daddy. Daddy. It's your play."

"Yes, honey, I'm coming." Ross looked at Johnny and a little of the man's force showed. "Can't help

134

you," he said. There was finality in the words, in the tone.

Johnny nodded. "Sorry I bothered you." He turned away and walked back to the lobby.

It was in Cottage B that he found Sonny and Betty March. "Just on our way to town," Sonny said, "but it can wait. Come on in." Sonny was happier than ever that he had flushed down the hotel john the white powder that had been in the plastic bag. He felt free, untouchable. "You know my wife, lieutenant?"

They sat in the pleasant sitting room of the cottage. "It's a tacky little place," Betty said, "not at all like Cottage A where we always stay. Cottage A has a view and that nice corner fireplace and it's closer to the Lodge so when it rains or snows—"

"Honey." There was weariness in Sonny's voice. "Leave it lay. It's only a few days. Why raise a stink?" He smiled at Johnny. "No sense in making waves, isn't that right, lieutenant?"

It was not exactly the attitude Johnny had always associated with Sonny March who was big, rich, Anglo, and quite used to having his own way. No matter. "A man named Wilson," he said, "Walter Wilson." He sat quiet, waiting.

Sonny frowned thoughtfully. Then he shook his head. "Sorry," he said. "The name doesn't ring a bell."

Johnny nodded as if that was the answer he had expected. "You stayed in the same motel down in Tucson last December," he said. "That could have been pure coincidence, of course." He paused. "But he was your dinner guest here at the Lodge maybe two weeks later, and I should think you might remember that."

Sonny was still frowning. It was Betty who said brightly, "Of course, honey, that nice little man we met in Tucson. He said he was coming to Santo Cristo and we told him to look us up and he came out for dinner and you and he talked for the longest time, don't you remember?" She paused for a quick breath. "We were in Cottage A then," she said to Johnny.

Sonny's frown cleared. "Got it," he said. "Sure, I remember him now. What about him, lieutenant?"

"Do you mind telling me what you and Wilson talked about?"

Sonny shrugged. "Just talk, I guess. You know, you meet somebody and you talk about all kinds of things, like—"

"You said it was business," Betty said. "I remember. I wanted to see that movie in town, the one everybody was talking about, a very adult film, the *New York Times* said, which probably meant that everybody took their clothes off and used dirty words everybody knows anyway, but the critic, I think it was Judith Crist, said it was powerful." Breath. "But you said you had to talk business with Mr. Wilson."

"I had to say something," Sonny said, "because I didn't want to drive into town to see the damned picture. I've seen naked women before." He spoke to Betty, but he kept his eyes on Johnny's face.

Johnny said, "What kind of business, Mr. March?"

"I told you. It was—"

"I heard," Johnny said. "But what kind of business did you and Wilson talk about?"

Sonny looked at his wife. He sighed. "You have attributes, doll, but sometimes you do keep them hidden.'' Then, to Johnny, ''Wilson traveled. Don't ask me who for, because I don't know, but he got around. All over the country. And sometimes outside. You know, Mexico, the Caribbean, not Cuba, but Haiti, the Dominican Republic, Jamaica, Puerto Rico—''

''Is that why we island-hopped for almost three months?'' Betty said. ''Never staying still long enough to even get really unpacked? I didn't even get a decent tan.''

''Baby,'' Sonny said, ''why don't you take a walk or powder your nose or wait in the car or something? I'll never get through if you don't quit interrupting.''

Betty wrinkled her nose at him.

''Look, lieutenant,'' Sonny said, ''I'll level with you. When you travel like we do, you like to pick things up, you know, things you see that you like, you buy them.''

Johnny nodded. He said nothing.

''Those damned restrictions they have now,'' Sonny said. ''You can only bring in so much duty-free and only once every six months, or maybe it's a year, it doesn't make any difference, it's a drag.''

Johnny nodded again in silence.

''I don't say Wilson talked about ways of getting things in without paying duty on them,'' Sonny said. ''But we did talk about this port-of-entry and that one, and how some places they shook you right down to your underwear—''

''They do, too,'' Betty said. ''They made me strip once, never mind where it was, strip all the way. They thought I had something in my bra. Actually! And the only things that were there was me.'' Pause. ''Were me?'' Another pause. ''I was all that was there.''

Sonny smiled. "Fact," he said. "Not that you can really blame them, the way she looks." Then, "That's what we talked about mostly, lieutenant. Care to tell me why you're interested?"

"Because Wilson's dead," Johnny said. "Somebody murdered him."

Betty said, "Oooh!"

Sonny snapped his fingers. "That's the name Mark Hawley mentioned at the barbecue. I've got it tied together now. He was under the snow, wasn't he?"

"He was," Johnny said, and wished that Mark Hawley had not mentioned the name. Forewarned, forearmed; wasn't there a Latin phrase for that? But maybe it wouldn't have made any difference. Sonny's story sounded real, and maybe it was, at that.

On the other hand, he thought as he drove without haste back into town, there was that anomaly that had struck him in the first part of their conversation; and anomalies were best checked out. He perched on Tony Lopez's desk. "Sonny March," he said. "What do you know about him?"

"Don't tell me he's got problems," Tony said. "I should have his problems. He's young and healthy and loaded, with a wife—" He shook his head. "I saw her once at the Lodge pool in a bikini. *Valgame Dios!* The kind of big knockers some Anglos have. They stick straight out." He indicated with a gesture how Betty's breasts stuck straight out.

Johnny had to smile. "Customs once thought she was smuggling something in her bra."

"Melons," Tony said. "Those big green ones.

There's plenty of room." He paused and studied Johnny's face. "What about Sonny March?"

Such a little thing, really; but was it? "They always stay in Cottage A at the Lodge," Johnny said. "Apparently it's the best cottage. But this time there's a man named Ross with his wife and daughter in Cottage A, and Betty March doesn't like it a bit that they have to stay in Cottage B, but Sonny says there's no point in raising a stink, making waves." He was silent.

Tony said slowly, "Hombre, are we talking about the same fellow?"

"Spell that out."

Tony leaned back in his chair. "Sonny March," he said, "is an arrogant Anglo son of a bitch when he doesn't get his own way. You meet him, he's nice enough, but cross him and he turns mean, you know the kind? Emilio, a cousin of mine, works for Sam Christopher, and Emilio says that if Sam Christopher could bring himself to turn down the money Sonny March spends at the Lodge, he wouldn't even let him near the place. Anything isn't the way Sonny wants it, he eats Sam Christopher's ass out and doesn't care who hears him doing it."

"Then," Johnny said, "why does he take Cottage B and his wife's complaints lying down?"

Tony thought about it. He said at last, "Who is this fellow Ross? Is that the reason?"

"I don't know," Johnny said. Simple truth. He tucked the anomaly away for later consideration.

He brought it out again that night, and presented it to Cassie. The matter of Paul Harper still hung between them, but by tacit consent they avoided it. Other subjects they could talk over as before. Or almost. "You asked a question one night, chica," Johnny said, "do you remember? You asked if all the higher-ups in organized crime looked and acted like Edward G. Robinson, or if maybe some of them seemed just ordinary, had wives and children, stayed at places like the Lodge." He paused. "That might explain why Sonny March—"

"Johnny." Cassie was shaking her head. "Johnny, don't you see? Sonny March would have to know who Mr. Ross is if he were somebody to be afraid of, and how would Sonny know?"

No, Johnny thought, it wasn't the same even on other subjects than Paul Harper. "Maybe," he said.

"Johnny." Cassie's voice was soft. She laid her hand on his arm. "Johnny, don't be paranoid. Don't find the Mafia coming at you from all directions. You've built a structure of suspicion—" She shook her head. She said then, "A man named Snyder came to see Paul this afternoon. Who is he?"

Johnny looked at her in silence.

"Who is he, Johnny? And why is he here?"

"Didn't Harper ask?"

Cassie was silent for a few moments. "He said he was from the Treasury Department. That means taxes. Is that what you're trying to do, Johnny, bring pressure on Paul that way just because you don't like him?"

"I've never met him, chica." Anger was stirring. He held it down with difficulty.

"It isn't fair, Johnny."

"Somebody else said that." Johnny paused. "María Victoria Sanchez. She said it wasn't fair when I told her that if she didn't talk, we might have more men dead from bad dope. I told her fair had nothing to do with it.'' He paused again. ''And that's what I'm telling you. Snyder doesn't have anything to do with taxes. He's a narco, a narcotics agent, and I didn't push him at your Paul Harper. I told him what I found out about those motels and let him make up his own mind.''

Cassie was silent, obviously troubled.

''But,'' Johnny said, ''if you ask me why Snyder's here, that's something else again.'' There was a kind of luxury in letting the anger loose. ''Do you want to ask that?''

''Why is he here, Johnny?''

''Because I asked for him. Because seven men are dead and their deaths are all tied together—''

''You can't be sure of that.''

''Chica,'' Johnny said, ''I'll stake my life on it.'' He stood up. Chico stood up too and looked from one human to the other, his black nose working, searching for comprehension. Johnny said, ''Until this is over, settled one way or another, we aren't going to agree on much of anything.''

''Johnny—''

''Tell your friend Harper,'' Johnny said, ''that I'll be around to see him one of these days.'' He walked across the room and out into the night, closing the door gently behind him.

14

Where Ben Hart's road met the highway, Mark Hawley turned in and drove rattling over the cattle guard. Off to his right the bulk of Cloud Mesa pushed against the clear sky; holy land, still possessed and worshiped by the nearby Pueblo Indians. The congressman remembered the long discussions that had preceded permission for Cassie Enright's dig on top of the mesa. Beyond the mesa the mountains stretched endlessly, their bald tops snow-covered still.

The sun was warm through the windshield, but the air against the congressman's cheek was cool. It was a strange land filled with contradictions and extremes. There were those who loved it, and those who could not abide it; there were very few with feelings in-between.

For more years than he cared to remember, the congressman had known this country; he was intimate with its vagaries, its secrets, its dangers. In its vastness a man could lose himself or take a crippling fall, and not be found until it was far too late. Men had, and not all that long ago, either.

In a straight line from Ben's ranch to the southeast, as the congressman well knew, there was no natural surface water for sixty miles, and when sometimes, as now, he thought about the early Europeans pushing on and on without maps or reliable information of any kind, he could only wonder at their audacity.

Given the chance, the sun that now felt pleasantly warm on his chest could desiccate you. In any of the small arroyos, dry as dry for months on end and sometimes years, a flash flood could come romping down from the mountains without warning, in its fury carrying rocks too heavy for a man to lift; and whole families camping in a sandy sheltered bottom had ended far from their camping spot, battered, dead. There were winds and dust-storms and in winter blizzards that swept in piling drifts higher than a man could reach in temperatures that had to be experienced to be believed: what was it only last January, twenty-three below zero at Ben's main ranch house, and the snow flying horizontal as if blown from a gun?

But these little items, as the congressman knew, were never mentioned in the ads that ran in Eastern papers and magazines offering land for sale, only $10, $50, $100 a month—although the number of months was also unmentioned.

The hell of it was, the congressman thought, that in a matter like this land development he was of two minds, and if there was one thing he prided himself on it was his ability to make decisions. He detested fence-straddling, but what was a man to do?

Sitting in Ben's big living room, a glass of bourbon in hand, he put it this way: "I've always held that a man, goddam it, ought to be able to take care of himself. You have. I have." He shook his head. "But it won't wash, and I know it, and you probably know it too. Some folks have to be led by the hand or they get lost, protected from other folks or they get fleeced, told what to do and how to do it or they just sit down and cry. Now isn't that a hell of a thing?"

Ben agreed that it was a hell of a thing. He smiled to himself.

"Stop that goddam smirking," the congressman said. "I haven't made up my mind yet." He had a sip of his whiskey. "I saw you twisting arms at the barbecue. How'd you make out?"

Ben shrugged his massive shoulders. "Hard to tell."

"It's nothing new," the congressman said. "Land speculators have been selling dreams ever since this country began." He shook his head. "But we're down to hardrock now." He gestured at the big windows framing the piñon-and-juniper growth dotting the nearby brown land. "Take a piece of ground that will maybe support a jackrabbit, two horny toads, and a kangaroo mouse, and what you say about it to folks back East who don't know any better is that the air is clear and the sun shines and there's ample room for kids to romp and the old folks to sit and watch the sunsets all orange and purple and gold. Just sign here."

Ben said, "Are you trying to convince me?"

The congressman set his whiskey down. "Harper," he said. "I've never met him, but I'm beginning to dislike him. No reason. Just hunch. I've asked a few

questions about him. Maybe we'll get some answers."
He paused. "Cassie Enright's working for him." There
was little that went on in the entire northern half of the
state that missed the congressman's attention.

"I told her to," Ben said. "Maybe she can talk sense
into him."

The congressman snorted. "Sometimes," he said,
"you behave like a reasonably sensible fellow. Other
times you don't seem to have the brains God gave a
Gila monster. If what I think may be true, nobody is
going to talk any sense into Harper except maybe with
the business end of a thirty-thirty." He paused. "Suppose what's behind Harper is the kind of money that
built some of those hotels in Nevada, in Miami Beach?"

Ben thought about it. "Whose idea is that?"

"Johnny Ortiz's."

Ben thought about it a little more. "That might alter
things some," he said. "Somebody might get skinned
up." He heaved himself out of his chair and went to
stand for a time in front of the fireplace. "Suppose
you're right," he said at last. "Then what?" He turned
to face the room again. "You've spent all those years
in Washington where near as I get it nobody ever means
what he says. You're used to looking behind the double-
talk. What comes after Harper's development?"

There was no hesitation. "We're a piss-poor state,"
the congressman said, "with a lot of space between
people. Fifth in size, thirty-seventh in population. By
and large, money will buy you more here than in most
places because there aren't many bidders. I don't know
what those people have in mind if they have anything
at all, but if I were running the show and didn't care

who got skinned up or how bad, I know what I might aim at."

Ben stood silent, waiting.

"We've got mountains for skiing," the congressman said, "for hunting, fishing; lakes for boating. We've got spreads like yours to turn into fancy dude ranches. With money and the leverage money can give you if you don't care how you use it, this area around Santo Cristo could be turned into the damndest tourist resort you ever saw, winter, summer, all year round." He paused. "Wide open. With everything. Gambling, prostitution, anything you want in the way of action. Las Vegas all over again, and I don't mean Las Vegas, New Mexico."

Ben walked back to his chair and sat down. He picked up his whiskey glass, studied it, and then set it back on the table untasted. He looked up. "So?"

"It's no skin off your ass," the congressman said. "I know that. When you come right down to it, it's no skin off mine, either. I can retire any time and get along just fine." He raised his hand. "Goddam it, let me finish." Pause. "I'm not necessarily wholly for motherhood and against sin no matter what I say when I'm campaigning. And I'd sooner sit and talk and have a drink with a whorehouse madam like Flora Hobbs any time than even be in the same room with a lot of respectable folks I know. I've never turned my back yet on a good poker game, and I'd hate to have to count the times I've been down on my knees with a pair of dice in my hand. I sure as hell don't object to nightclub shows featuring topless girls with big tits." Another pause. "But, like I said, some folks have to be looked after because they can't see farther than their noses and if somebody waves a fast buck in front of them they jump at it." A third pause. "That's part of it. I'm in the habit of looking out for those folks."

"What's the rest of it?" Ben said, although he thought he already knew the answer.

"I don't like to be pushed around," the congressman said. "I don't like being lied to, either, but not because of the morality involved. When a man lies to me I resent it because he's insulting my intelligence; he thinks he's putting something over on me. And if this land development Harper is promoting has something behind it other than it appears, then I'm being lied to *and* pushed around and there's going to be some fur flying before it's all over."

Ben sighed. "All right," he said. "What do we do?"

"I don't know yet. It wants thinking about. And maybe Johnny's wrong and there's nothing fishy going on at all. Maybe." The congressman picked up his whiskey glass and sniffed it appreciatively. "I just wanted to see if you wanted to sit in if anything gets started." He nodded. "Being the contrary kind of son of a bitch you are, I was pretty sure you would." He raised the glass. *"Salud."*

Ben reached for his own glass.

Cassie drove out to the property Harper was promoting. It was west of town, adjacent to Ben Hart's holdings; gently rolling land cut here and there by small arroyos, dotted with cholla, piñon, juniper, chamisa, and grama grass. There was no natural surface water, and, as yet, no roads beyond the single piece of blacktop that led a hundred yards in from the highway beneath a fake adobe arch bearing raised letters: RAVEN ESTATES.

Cassie left her car at the end of the blacktop and began to walk. She had no destination, merely a desire to absorb the feel of the land, to try to visualize it as a populated community.

She could not fault the location, the view of Cloud Mesa and the mountains. The land was exposed, and like the congressman Cassie was well aware of the ferocity of the weather that could come sweeping in. But trees could be planted for windbreaks, houses could be oriented, and walls could be built to shelter patios; with planning, discomfort from the weather could be kept to a minimum.

And the sky was clear, limitless; only a faint brownish line of haze following the distant river valley gave proof of the pollution poured into the atmosphere from the great power plants two hundred miles away. Compared to Eastern cities, Cassie thought, this was unpolluted heaven. Still.

Water. That was the item on which all else depended. With water the land could be made to bloom and anything was possible; without it nothing could be done. Ben Hart had drilled his wells, filled his stock tanks, even given nature a hand over near the mountains and guided snow run-off into catch basins for summer use. Ben had enough water for his cattle and his own use, but none to waste, and what could happen when Raven Estates became reality and dishwashers and washing machines and lawn sprinklers took over?

Hydrology, she told herself, was not her area of competence; that question could be left to others. And she knew that she was deliberately turning her back on what could not be avoided, hoping it would go away, which was a human enough reaction, but one which a few people spurned. Johnny, for example.

What brought Johnny to mind? Face it, she told herself, he's never been out of your mind. All right, then, why did they have to disagree? Because I have my pride and my sensitivities just as he has his. Explanation offered scant solace. Cassie kicked at a stone and watched it skitter off across the dirt. Damn, she thought, damn, damn, damn!

She walked on. Ahead was the familiar bulk of Cloud Mesa, sacred land. Had she profaned it with her dig? Now what in the world raised that question which she had never even considered before? Of course she had not profaned it. And yet, in a way, she had. Just by being there, supervising a dig, searching into the distant past?

No; her thoughts suddenly took a strange, circuitous direction. The profanity lay in her being what she was, a stranger, unbelieving, using the sacred land for her own purposes. A ridiculous concept, but at the moment to her it was very real. Why?

She stopped walking and looked around. Was there a parallel? Was that the conclusion she was trying to reach? Was Paul Harper, using this land for his own purposes, somehow committing a similar offense? Against whom? Or against what?

"How silly can you be?" She asked the question aloud, and heard no reply. She turned slowly, looking in all directions. There was only emptiness. She could scream, she thought, and no one would hear. She could die, and no one would know. She found no fear in the concept.

Lonely land, she thought; lovely, lonely land. Maybe that was what troubled her. "I would hate to see it changed," she said. "There would be the profanity."

She turned away then and walked back to her car, her mind at ease at last.

15

Snyder the narcotics man sat again in Johnny's office. "Your congressman asked a couple of questions," he said, and smiled. "That's how it goes sometimes, a simple little question and before you're finished answering it you've poked into dark corners you didn't even know were there." He took out a folded paper, opened it. "Are you ready?"

Johnny felt a faint prickling in his scalp, the kind of sensation that sometimes meant the quarry was near; not always, of course, but often enough that you paid it heed when, say, on a trail you felt it and you slowed and went cautiously around the next bend and there, sure enough, was that bull elk you'd been following, right in the middle of an open meadow, looking big as the side of a barn. He kept his face and his voice expressionless. "Let's have it," he said.

"Raven Estates Development Corporation," Snyder read, "is a wholly owned subsidiary of Sly Investors, Inc." He paused, smiling again. "Sly isn't a pun. There was a man named Sly who built up a sizeable fund concentrating on New York real estate. Then he made a couple of wrong guesses and the bubble collapsed. An outfit called Midtown Enterprises bailed Sly out and ended up owning Sly Investors. Midtown Enterprises backs shows both on-and-off-Broadway, owns and runs a couple of restaurants, owns at least one Manhattan hotel, and has a piece of three national motel chains.''

Johnny sat up straighter. ''Which chains?''

''You have a good eye,'' Snyder said. ''The chains that include the motels in Tucson, Phoenix, and El Paso where Wilson and Harper stayed. They may also have a piece of the Mid-Towner Motor Hotel here in Santo Cristo, but that isn't hard intelligence.'' He went back to his paper. ''Midtown Enterprises, incidentally, has some interesting people on its board, including a New Jersey mayor long suspected of racket affiliations, and an ex-New York congressman, very prominent fellows. The New Yorker is an *ex*-congressman because there was more than suspicion that he was playing fast and loose with his congressional influence and he decided not to run for re-election to avoid any big fuss.'' Snyder looked up from the paper. ''Do you want more? It's a jungle only corporate lawyers and tax accountants could work their way through.'' He looked at the paper once more. ''There's a big travel agency, a pharmaceutical house, a small Gulf Coast shipping line, and hotels in San Juan, Miami Beach, and Las Vegas, all at least partially tied in. It is, in short, friend, a large-sized operation.''

It was, indeed. Johnny thought about it with awe. He was no businessman; he didn't even know how interlocking corporations operated, and he decided that he had been happy in his ignorance. On the other hand, the tip of this iceberg had surfaced right here in his own town, and that meant that at least part of its doings was his business. "Who runs all this?" he said.

Snyder folded the paper and tucked it away. "Hard to tell. What is probably the ultimate policy-making company specializes in estate management, all open and aboveboard, and there's a list of their officers who may or may not actually pull the strings. Unless you can sit in on board meetings you don't know for sure who makes the decisions and who just listens and nods. But a man named Ross—"

Johnny pounced on the name. "Peter Ross?"

"That's his name. Lives in Westchester. Married. Has a daughter about to enter Wellesley. Sails an International class sloop, plays tennis, fences at the New York Athletic Club, is active in charity drives, and is rumored to carry a lot of weight in the estate-management company that may pull the strings for all the rest." Snyder paused, unsmiling now. "Like I said, a jungle. That doesn't necessarily mean it's organized crime. A lot of so-called conglomerates are just as complicated and wouldn't dream of doing anything as blatant as distributing heroin or seeing to it that an occasional nuisance turns up dead." He paused again. "But if there are huge profits from organized crime, and there are, then the money has to get into something legitimate in order to be of any use and not attract too much attention, and this kind of tinker-toy structure put together by very smart lawyers and accountants is precisely the kind of thing illegal money can be fed into and passed around until it loses all identity."

"You know," Johnny said, "I don't think I'd like to change jobs with you." Simple truth; the meticulous paperwork routine was not his way, nor would it have been suited to a town like Santo Cristo where most crime sprang from simple causes, and personalities counted for a great deal more than hidden complications. Most times, that was. "Did you happen to pick up anything on Harper?"

"I went to see him."

"I heard." Johnny kept his voice deliberately noncommittal.

"Reason was," Snyder said, "that I wanted to ask him about Sly Investors. He was happy to tell me what I already knew, and suggested that if it was a tax matter I'd do well to talk to the people back in New York." Snyder paused. "I have some good fingerprints of his on the covers of the reports I showed him on Sly Investors. We'll see what the Bureau turns up in its files."

Johnny was smiling. Tracking, he thought; that was the name of the game; fingerprints, footprints, any conceivable trace that someone might leave as a trail to follow, these were the signposts. "I'll be interested to hear," he said.

Cassie sat again in Harper's office. Distantly the cathedral bells sounded the hour, and she listened until they were done, conscious that Harper watched her curiously. "The cathedral has been here quite a while," she said in partial explanation. "Not back to Santo Cristo's beginnings, of course, but long enough so that it is part of the whole scene."

"I'm not sure I understand you."

Cassie took her time. "Change here comes slowly," she said at last. "I guess that's what I'm trying to say, Paul. In some places change comes all at once as a snake changes his skin. Every time I see Los Angeles it's as if it has rebuilt itself from the ground up. Not true, of course, but that is the feeling I get." She paused. "But here change comes gradually, and there is time to absorb the new into the old, or at least we like to think it happens that way. People go away and come back years later and Santo Cristo is as they remember it. It isn't, of course, but the atmosphere hasn't altered, and that is the important thing."

Harper leaned back in his chair. "First," he said, "you told me you weren't earning your pay. Now you are trying to tell me—what?"

Cassie faced him squarely. "I don't want to see change, sudden change. I don't want to see blacktop roads and planted windbreaks and patio walls and row after row of houses in that lovely, lonely emptiness." Cassie paused. "I'm sorry, Paul. I don't want any pay. I haven't done anything to earn it. I never should have taken on anything except my own work which is poking into the past, not trying to mess around with the future." She stopped and spread her hands. "There it is."

There was silence. Harper said at last, "I wish you would change your mind."

"I'm sorry."

Harper picked up a pencil, studied it, set it down again very gently. Damn the woman, anyway, he thought; but his face showed nothing. He said, "Has somebody been—persuading you?"

"It isn't that," Cassie said. She thought of Johnny. "At least, not entirely."

"What does that mean?"

"I'm trying to be honest," Cassie said. "I'm not good at evasion. I've heard—never mind what I've heard, because I don't believe it." Then why does it stick in your mind, Cassandra? Because it was Johnny who said it, why else? "And," she said, "since I don't believe it, it has nothing to do with my decision, nothing at all." The small voice in her mind said: Oh, brother, the things you can pretend to believe! Where has the fine objective scientific detachment fled, Cassandra?

"What things have you heard, Cassie?"

"It doesn't matter."

"If these things concern me," Harper said, "don't I have a right to know them?"

Did he not? Cassie thought about it, and the only possible conclusion was that he did have a right to know. Always her sympathies were with the hunted, with the deer fleeing in the woods, with the rabbit when the coyote pursued. But why should these examples come to mind now? Had she already accepted Johnny's theories and conclusions? In the questions was confusion, and in confusion exasperation. "When you were down in Arizona and Texas last December," she began, and wondered how to end the sentence.

"Specifically in Tucson, Phoenix, and El Paso," Harper said, "with in-between a quick trip to Mexico City, yes." There was nothing in his voice, or in his manner beyond ordinary puzzlement. "What about it?

Am I supposed to have done something wicked?'' He was smiling.

It sounded ridiculous, Cassie thought, and probably was. Hundreds of people had stayed at those same three motels, and just because this one had been among them he was suspect. Did that make any sense at all? ''Did you know a man named Walter Wilson?'' she said.

Harper said slowly, wonderingly, ''Did I know—?'' He stopped. ''That's the man they found under the snow, isn't it? Up at the ski basin?'' He watched Cassie nod. ''I don't get it,'' Harper said. ''First you talk about Tucson and Phoenix and El Paso, and then you jump to the ski basin here at Santo Cristo. Where's the connection?'' He paused. ''Or is there a connection?''

''I don't know,'' Cassie said. She hesitated. ''Except that Walter Wilson stayed in the same motels you did.'' There. It was out, and as she watched Harper's pitying smile and slow headshake, she thought that it had been a long time since she had felt quite this foolish.

''Someone,'' Harper said, ''is going far out.'' The smile faded. ''I wonder why.''

Cassie shook her head in silence. That small voice was clamoring again in her mind. She tried to ignore it.

''Cassie,'' Harper said. ''Cassie. Look at me. What kind of a monster am I supposed to be? Do you see horns? Cloven hooves? What am I supposed to have done?''

It was all mere theory, suspicion, not a trace of real evidence. Not true, Cassandra. There was one indication that was more than sheer guesswork, and to salvage some of her pride she brought it forth. "The Treasury man," she said.

"Snyder?" Harper's eyes narrowed almost imperceptibly. "What about him?"

"Did he say he was a tax man?"

Harper said slowly, "He didn't say. And I didn't ask." He paused. "But what else?"

"He's a narcotics man."

Harper put his forehead in his hand and let his breath out in a long sigh. Then he looked again at Cassie. His smile was bitter. "What will they think of next?" he said. "Flying saucers?"

"I'm sorry, Paul." What else was there to say?

It was pure hunch, of course, and at this point if Johnny had been asked to justify it, he would have been hard pressed for any explanation other than hope. To Tony Lopez he said, "If we don't have a picture of Harper, the newspaper will. They've given enough space to that development of his."

Tony agreed that it was so. He wore a resigned expression. "And what am I to do with the photo when I have it? Show it where? Harper lives out in the open. It is probable that he has a supermarket he shops at, and a drug store, a garage to tend his car, a liquor store—" He looked at Johnny and spread his hands. "Instruct me, amigo."

"Our friend Mary Margaret McDade," Johnny said. "Has she ever seen Harper going into the dirty movie house? If she has, does she remember when? Recently? Or maybe a few months ago?"

"*Dios!*" Tony said.

"And the girl Judy at the theatre—does she recognize Harper as a theatre customer?"

Tony was shaking his head sadly. So simple, he thought, but it had taken an intuitive jump even to see the possibility. *"A tus órdenes,"* he said, "at thy service."

"One thing more," Johnny said, and then corrected himself: "Two things. Does Harper know Peter Ross out at the Lodge? And does Harper know Sonny March?"

Johnny sat at his own desk for a time after Tony had gone. Ideas were beginning to stir, but so far they were mere fantasy, interesting, even possible, but without foundation in fact. *If* the tinker-toy structure Snyder had described was indeed more than a complicated conglomerate put together for nothing more sinister than tax shenanigans; and *if* Peter Ross was in fact the main force in the estate-management company which called the shots all the way down the line through Midtown Enterprises, Sly Investors, and all the others; and *if* some of the money that filtered down to Raven Estates Development Corporation had come from, say, heroin distribution and sales, then a number of possibilities were immediately opened up.

Paul Harper *could* be as innocent as he appeared, merely a specialist in real estate development brought in to get Raven Estates under way. In an organization as vast as the one Snyder had described, there had to be numbers of innocent people merely working at jobs and knowing nothing of what went on around them. But if Harper was innocent, how then to explain the coincidences of his visits to three motels only a few days before Wilson appeared?

There was a possible explanation, of course, although Johnny hated to admit it: Midtown Enterprises owned stock in the chains to which each of the three motels belonged. It was likely that employees of subsidiary organizations would stay in affiliated hostelries, no? Then how explain the closeness of the dates? More important, how explain the coincidence of death by poisoned heroin in each city so soon after Harper's departure? Balls.

You are, Juan Felipe, Johnny told himself, finding bull elk tracks on bare rock just because you want them to be there. The reason? Cassie, what else? And at this point the telephone rang and even before he picked it up he knew who it was. "Hi, chica," he said. His voice was gentle.

There was a short silence. Then, "You knew, Johnny?" Cassie's voice.

"I knew. And don't ask me how. I was thinking of you. *Qué pasa?*"

It was a simple enough thing that she had to say, and it could easily have been said on the telephone, but she wanted to see Johnny's face when she told him, and so she said, "Will you meet me?"

"Any place. Any time."

"The plaza," Cassie said, and added without knowing why, "in the sunshine."

The sun was warm, the air was clear and dry, and they were smiling as they approached each other along the flagstone path. They stopped, and made no move even to shake hands. "Let's sit here," Johnny said. He indicated the low wall. Perched, he watched Cassie, and waited.

"I just wanted to tell you," Cassie said, "that I've stopped doing any work for Raven Development." She saw no change in his face, but deep in his eyes she was sure there was an expression of satisfaction. It was warming.

"Tell me why, chica."

He listened as she told him what she had told Harper about not wanting to see change in the lonely land. "Is that the only reason?" Johnny said.

"I—don't know. I think so." Some of the exasperation remained: why did he have to press her for explanation?

"Or," Johnny said, "were there—vibrations you didn't like?" He paused, saw resistance forming, and added quickly, "I need to know, chica. I have too many questions, too few answers. You can help."

The exasperation faded. "I don't know," she said. "I haven't anything against Paul." True? Examine that statement, Cassandra. You resented him the first time you saw him. The second time he buttered you up, and you've thought him a fine fellow ever since. Still? "At least, I don't think I have," she said. Her eyes went across the plaza where Harper was walking slowly. He saw her; of that she was positive. But he did not wave.

Johnny, turning to follow her glance, said, "That's the fellow?" And then, looking again at Cassie, "He doesn't look too friendly. What did you tell him, chica? Just that you had changed your mind?"

"Oh," Cassie said, "it was—silly." She hesitated. What she had told Harper no longer seemed quite so innocuous, and that was silly too. Unless, she thought, unless she was beginning to believe Johnny's structure of suspicion? She sat silent for a few moments digesting the implications of that, and liking them not.

Johnny watched her, and waited.

"I told him," Cassie said, "about the motels in Tucson, Phoenix, and El Paso, and that you knew Walter Wilson stayed there too." She hesitated. "Was that wrong? Was it, Johnny?" Why, oh why, she asked herself, didn't you stick strictly to anthropology and the past, Cassandra? You are a babe in the woods in the present.

Johnny was showing the white teeth in a smile. "Probably it was wrong, chica," he said. The smile spread. "But that is precisely the kind of thing that sometimes makes somebody move when he'd much rather sit still." The smile faded. "But I'd rather it was somebody else than you who told him."

For only a moment she felt a little shiver, as of cold. Someone walking over my grave, she thought. "Why, Johnny? What difference?"

"Leave it to us," Johnny said. He showed the white teeth again. "And in case you've got women's lib ideas that we think we're smarter than you, forget them. It's just that if you're going to try to flush a bear out of a berry patch, you'd better make sure you're ready if he comes out the wrong way. He may be a grizzly, and he may be mean." He turned again to glance at Harper's distant back. Then, to Cassie once more, "I'll go have a talk with him, chica." He raised his hand to forestall protest. "All friendly." The smile disappeared. "But

I want him to know that you're my girl, and if anything—"

"Am I, Johnny? Still?"

"*Siempre,* always." Johnny's voice was solemn. "Nothing changes that, chica." He paused. "Except your choice."

She could have laughed aloud, or, boots, Levis, and all, gone into a whirling dance. Had it really gone this deep, the rift between them and the feeling that it might not be bridged? Here in the relief she felt was the answer. "Then," she said, "*siempre* is the word."

16

It seemed to Tony Lopez that the girl at the porno movie house, whose name was Judy, had changed some since he had last seen her. Her eyelashes were longer, her skirt was shorter, and, he was pretty sure, her breasts pushed a little harder against the sweater. He objected to none of the changes, and he took a little time to appraise them.

Judy bore the examination with equanimity. "If you're going to buy a ticket," she said, "which I bet you aren't—"

"There is a sentence," Tony said. He was smiling. "It isn't even finished, *guapa,* and already it's clear off the reservation. I'm not going to buy a ticket." He held out the picture of Paul Harper. "Know him?" He watched the girl's face carefully.

The long eyelashes fluttered briefly, but when the girl looked up from the photo her face was expressionless and her voice perfectly steady. "Should I?"

"That," Tony said, "isn't an answer." He waited quietly, large and solid.

Judy hesitated. Then, "I don't think I've ever seen him." Her eyes searched Tony's face. It was evident she was trying denial on for size. It was equally evident that she saw it did not fit. "I suppose," she said, "that that cow in the junk shop says she's seen him here."

"Could be," Tony said.

"Then why ask me?"

Why, indeed? But the answer was perfectly clear: because that Indian *brujo* Johnny Ortiz had said to. Period. "I'm still asking," Tony said.

The girl squared her shoulders and thrust her breasts out aggressively. "So, okay," she said. "I've probably seen him here. I've seen a lot of guys here. That's what we're in business for, in case you didn't know." She paused. "Or didn't your mother tell you that guys like to look at girls without their clothes on? It's called sex."

Tony was puzzled. Why all the heat? he wondered. Had Johnny anticipated this? How? Why? No matter; if there was one thing Tony had learned from J. Ortiz it was that in an investigation anything out of the ordinary was to be pursued. Obliquely, if possible. "Maybe you remember when he's been here?" he said. His voice was mild, pleasant. He thought he saw relief in the girl's eyes. Why?

"He was here last week," she said. "Thursday. Thursday night. So?"

"It must be a strain standing like that," Tony said. "Relax, *guapa*. I've seen what you have." Now why should she remember the exact night? Never mind now. Leave it, and come back later. "He's a regular customer?"

The girl relaxed her shoulders. She said slowly, "You're a real son of a bitch, aren't you?"

"Sometimes." Nothing showed in Tony's face. "My question?"

"He comes here sometimes."

"How long has he been coming?"

"How would I know?"

"How do you remember he was here Thursday night? Not Wednesday, not Friday, Thursday?" Of course, of course. "Do you know his name?"

"Why would I—?" The girl stopped. "What if I do?" she said. "It's been in the papers, hasn't it?"

"But," Tony said gently, "I'll bet you didn't learn it from the newspapers. He's a friend of yours, is he, honey?"

"That," Judy said, "is none of your damn business."

"I could make it my business. We have ways, you know."

The girl studied him. Rebellion had flared; it subsided now. "You'd love that, wouldn't you. You're all alike. You just love waving muscle. Just because you carry a badge—"

"You're wrong," Tony said. "I don't love it, honey. I don't even like it particularly." He paused. "But I do it when I have to." He paused again. "When what I'm trying to find out is important, then I lean just as hard as it's necessary, even on pretty girls with big tits." A third pause. "Understood?"

The long eyelashes lowered and then slowly lifted again. The girl was silent, defeated.

"Bueno," Tony said, "now we begin at the beginning."

He drove straight back to headquarters from the theatre and went into Johnny's office to lean against the wall. Studying Johnny, he began to smile. "You look, amigo," he said, "like my sister Angelina's cat after she got the goldfish." He held up one hand quickly. "Okay," he said, "okay. I won't push it." He watched Johnny relax, even smile. Funny, Tony thought. A year ago he wouldn't have dared make a quip at the Indian's expense; and even now you didn't go too far, but it was a hell of a lot easier, nevertheless. "The girl Judy at the skin-flick house," he said, and recounted the conversation.

Johnny listened with interest, everything else set aside.

"You've seen her," Tony said. "A good-looking chick. Stacked. It wasn't hard to guess how it is. Guys who come to look at the skin-flicks see her and she waves those tits at them, and maybe they get the idea that they'd like a little action. Judy's willing. It, like they say, supplements her income."

Johnny nodded.

"Nobody's hurt," Tony said, "and I'm sure as hell not going to haul her in for prostitution, but it was a lever to use, no?"

"Yes," Johnny said without hesitation.

Tony went on. "Harper's a customer of hers. She likes him. Maybe that's why she had a little trouble remembering, but finally she did." Tony paused. "The first time she saw him," he said, "was the day of the big snow." He was silent.

Johnny said slowly, "The day Wilson was killed, and Warren found him and took him up to the ski slope." He nodded. "You're sure." It was a statement, no question, but it demanded an answer.

"The reason I'm sure," Tony said, "is because he asked Judy to forget that he'd come there. Bad for public relations, he said, if people knew he went to watch dirty movies."

"But he was there Thursday night," Johnny said.

Tony shook his head. "He didn't go to the flick. He picked Judy up after they closed. She guessed that the McDade woman had seen Harper, and when, and she was just trying to throw me off by mentioning Thursday night." He paused. "Harper was only in the theatre once. That was the day of the big snow. McDade remembered that it was some time ago, but she couldn't pin it down to a day or even a week. Judy could. She did."

One more little piece, Johnny thought. It didn't prove anything; not in the sense that it was evidence that would stand up in court; but it did bring Harper and Wilson into proximity one more time, and that, to Johnny's mind, almost without question ruled out coincidence. He was suddenly aware that Tony had asked a question. "Do I still want to know if Harper knows Ross and March?" Johnny said. He nodded decisively. "Now more than ever." He pushed back his chair and stood up. "I think it's time I met Mr. Harper."

"You want company?"

"No." Johnny was smiling. "He's all mine."

There was nothing grand about Harper's office. Somehow, after hearing Snyder's report, Johnny had expected paneled walls and thick carpeting; but there was only a single, not very good Santo Domingo rug on the brick floor, and the walls were whitewashed adobe. Most of one wall was covered by a large plat showing Raven Estates complete with roads that had not yet been built curving among numbered lots. Johnny gave it more than a passing glance.

Harper said, "Interested in buying property, lieutenant?" He was easy, assured, even, apparently, faintly amused.

"Not at the moment," Johnny said. There was a chair and Harper had gestured toward it, but Johnny remained standing while he studied the man. He was good-sized, and looked to be in good physical shape. There was about him a quality Johnny had seen before in big-city Easterners, a kind of built-in sense of rectitude, a conviction that whatever he did was right and proper; no self-doubts showing. So.

Harper said, "I understand you are interested in my staying at motels in Tucson, Phoenix, and El Paso last winter."

"Does that amuse you?"

"It happens that I was there on business."

"That's a pretty broad word," Johnny said. "Mind if I ask what business?"

"Now, lieutenant," Harper smiled. "What I do is not exactly a secret." He nodded toward the plat on the wall. "But there are certain aspects of investigating the property and then arranging for its purchase and financing and other details that are best not broadcast. I don't know how much you know of these matters—"

"Very little," Johnny said.

Harper nodded. "Then you'll just have to take my word for it, lieutenant."

"Walter Wilson," Johnny said, and left it there.

"I didn't know him," Harper said. He smiled again. "Oh, yes, I recognize the name. It has been in the papers." True enough. "And," Harper said, "I recall that the police asked for any information anyone might have concerning him." He paused. "As a matter of curiosity, lieutenant, did anyone come forward?"

"Now, Mr. Harper," Johnny said, and smiled. "What I do is not exactly a secret. But there are certain aspects of an investigation that are best not broadcast. I'm sure you can appreciate that."

"A policeman with a sense of humor," Harper said. He shook his head in mock wonder.

"Cassie tells me," Johnny said, "that she is no longer doing work for Raven Estates."

"So she said." Harper was unsmiling now. "I'm hoping to persuade her to change her mind."

"Are you a persuasive fellow?"

"Sometimes. When I have to be."

"Some of my ancestors," Johnny said, "weren't exactly persuasive but they had their little ways of dealing with people who did things they didn't like."

"Such as, lieutenant?"

"Such as staking them out on ant hills."

The room was still. Harper said, "I'll bear it in mind, lieutenant."

"You do that."

"I'm being threatened?"

"No," Johnny said. "Just warned. This is my country and I know it pretty well. Maybe back in New York things would be different, but we aren't back in New York." He paused. There was no comment. "For someone who didn't know Walter Wilson," Johnny said then, "you seem to have come awful close to him quite a few times."

"Tucson, Phoenix, and El Paso again?" Harper was smiling. "We could put it to music, lieutenant." The smile disappeared. "For all I know, I could have been close to him here in Santo Cristo." He shrugged.

"You were."

Harper's eyebrows rose. "Indeed? Where? When?"

"The day of the big snow in January. At the porno movie house. You were both there that day. The film was about girl camps in Nazi Germany."

The man was good, Johnny thought. Nothing in his face changed. "You seem very sure of yourself, lieutenant," Harper said.

"I am." Johnny made a small gesture of dismissal. *"Hasta luego."* He walked out into the bright sunshine.

He did not go back to headquarters. Instead he walked to the museum to stand in the doorway of Cassie's small office. "Come for a ride with me, chica." He smiled down at the dog beside Cassie's feet. "You too," he said. Chico thumped the floor with his tail.

They rode in Johnny's pick-up, Chico on the seat between them, Johnny's rifle in the rack across the rear window. They took the ski basin road, and Cassie wondered what their destination might be, but did not ask. Anywhere, she thought, and was strangely content just jouncing up the mountain on the washboard road.

"You said I was seeing shadows," Johnny said, "organized crime under every bed."

"That was then. I—"

"No, chica, keep it that way." Johnny glanced at the smooth brown face. His voice was gentle. "Poke holes," he said, "because I'm going far out." He told Cassie of the girl Judy and her story that Harper had been in the theatre the day of the big snow. "In the theatre," Johnny repeated, "and only that once." He glanced again at Cassie's face. "Since then he's been seeing Judy. As a customer. Do you buy that?"

"Don't you? You say she's pretty, with a nice body—"

Johnny showed the white teeth. "And men will be men? Maybe. But suppose it isn't just sex? Suppose he has been deliberately making a play for the girl, going out of his way to make her like him, in order to keep her quiet? As far as he knows, she's the only one who could put him in the theatre the day Wilson was killed."

Cassie thought about it. "But she talked anyway."

"She had to," Johnny said, "for a reason Harper didn't know about: the McDade woman who spends her time watching who goes into the theatre. She's the reason Judy couldn't deny that Harper had ever been inside. And when Tony leaned on her and waved a prostitution charge in her face, any liking she had for Harper was outweighed."

"I don't know her," Cassie said slowly, "but I feel sorry for her. What's the phrase—victimless crimes? Isn't prostitution high on that list? Nobody's hurt. All the girl has to sell is her body. The man gets what he wants. Where's the harm? Flora's girls are no different."

Johnny nodded. "I won't argue." He was thinking of the two girls wrapped in blankets. Funny that should come to mind, except that it had been a kind of starting point. "But we use what levers we have, chica, if what we're after is important enough."

"I know." Cassie nodded sadly. Her hand stroked Chico's ear. "All right," she said, "let's assume that Paul was trying to keep the girl quiet. That shows that it's important, doesn't it, that nobody knows he was in the theatre that day? Important to him?"

Johnny swung the pick-up off the road and out on the scenic lookout parking area. He set the brake and switched off the engine. The silence was pleasant.

They were at 10,000 feet elevation and the vast country was spread before them. There was the city nestling in the foothills as it had for three and a half centuries. Yonder was the green line of the river swinging in a great curve at the foot of the western mountains. There on the horizon, a hundred miles away, in the clear dry air showing plainly the snow on its upper slopes, was Mount Taylor. Overhead the sky deepened in color toward its center. The sun pressed warmly through the windshield.

"If I'm right," Johnny said, "it was very important to him that nobody could place him in that theatre that day." He turned to look at Cassie. "And maybe if Judy had known how important it was, she wouldn't have talked no matter how hard Tony leaned on her." He shook his head. "But to her there's no connection with a dead man up on the ski slope. She thinks Wilson walked out of the theatre. We know he didn't."

Cassie closed her eyes briefly. She opened them again. "And," she said, "you think Paul killed him? Why?"

Johnny did not hesitate. "Presumably there was money in Wilson's belt. That could be one reason, but I don't think it's the main one." He rubbed his fingers gently on the steering wheel. "The poisoned heroin keeps coming to mind, chica, and I think it's more important than anything else. We don't know where it came from, but we know Wilson had it."

"And you're guessing," Cassie said, "that he was taking it back to the home office as proof that something was going on?" How easily she fell into Johnny's way of thought. Agreement? Or mere affection? "Do I have it right?" she said.

"Does it add up?"

Cassie hesitated. Slowly she nodded. "I think so."

"Then," Johnny said, "if Harper didn't want that poisoned heroin to get back to the home office, that could be his real reason for killing Wilson, no? He didn't get the dope because it was in the motel safe, but at least he stopped Wilson."

Cassie closed her eyes again. "Then you're saying," she said, "that the poisoned heroin was dangerous to Paul. And that can only mean that it was he who had it poisoned and he was responsible for the deaths in Tucson, Phoenix, and El Paso." She opened her eyes. "You're making him out to be a monster, aren't you?"

"Add Wilson's death," Johnny said, "and his score so far is four. You ask me why?" He shrugged. "They don't always come out neat and clean, chica. My guess is that there's an internal fight going on, an attempt at a take-over, and Harper is field man for the rebels." His fingers continued to rub lightly on the wheel, accompaniment to jumping thoughts. "I wish," he said, "I knew more about Peter Ross."

Chico wriggled and spoke, a small whimpering sound asking information concerning his two humans who were now so solemn.

"It's all right," Cassie said, and pulled the soft ears gently. She looked at Johnny. "If Peter Ross is what you make him out to be," she said, "he's—dangerous, Johnny. I don't know how such people behave, but—" She shook her head. Her face was troubled. I am convinced, she thought, and could not have said why.

"There's one other thing that has to tie in," Johnny said, "if only on the fringes—that bomb in Berry's shop. It was a professional job. Wilson's death was a professional job. It isn't likely that we have two different sets of professionals here in Santo Cristo. Suppose—" He paused and stared unseeing at the horizon. He said thoughtfully, "It was a warning. Suppose Berry got in the way, maybe tried an operation of his own, peddling a little dope on the side? The organization wouldn't take that quietly, would they?"

Cassie made one final attempt at disbelief. "You are really convinced," she said, "aren't you?"

Johnny faced her squarely. He was smiling, but the dark eyes were humorless. "Aren't you?"

Cassie shivered faintly. "Yes," she said with slow reluctance, "I'm afraid I am."

17

Peter Ross played tennis with his daughter Cindy on one of the Lodge's immaculate courts. "Better, honey," he said, "much better. Just remember to get down on your backhand, your hand lower than the racquet head. Then you have control of the shot."

"You're a perfectionist, daddy." The girl was smiling, proud.

"If a thing is worth doing—" Ross began.

"—it is worth doing well," Cindy said. They both laughed as they walked off the court.

"I think a shower," Ross said. "Then how about a swim? We'll see if your mother will come with us."

"Groovy." The girl hesitated. "This has been great, daddy, a real, you know, vacation. Oh, I know, we've got everything at home, but this is, you know, different."

"I know," Ross said. He saw Tony Lopez walk out of the main Lodge building and get into the police car, and a faint warning bell began to toll in his mind. Now what was that all about? Ross didn't like hunches, but sometimes you had the feeling that a situation was getting out of hand, that what ought to have been solid equilibrium was being unbalanced by forces you could not quite put your hands on. Wilson's death and disappearance were still very much a disturbing break in routine, and now police coming out here—

"Is anything wrong, daddy?"

"Not a thing, honey." Ross was smiling again.

Cindy had seen the police car driving off. "What do you suppose the fuzz was doing here?" she said.

"Probably something to do with a traffic ticket." Ross paused. "Or I suppose they have policemen's benefit balls out here too and he was selling tickets." He paused again. "Or," he said, smiling still, "maybe he came out to issue a warning, and we'll find it in our box."

"Warning?" The girl was frowning. "About what?"

"You. A girl as pretty as you is a traffic menace. Drivers can't keep their eyes on the road."

Cindy tucked her arm through his. She was smiling now. "Keep it up, daddy. I love it."

Now what was that cop doing here, anyway? Ross asked himself. The situation just did not feel right.

He came out of his shower, and then with sudden decision began to dress. Cindy, in a bikini, was waiting for him in the cottage sitting room. "Sorry, honey," Ross said, "I'm afraid I have to go into town. You and your mother swim." It was not often that he disappointed his womenfolk, and always when he did, as now, he felt a measure of guilt. But that faint warning bell was tolling, and long ago he had discovered that it was well not to ignore its clamor.

He drove into town, parked, and found a public telephone booth. He could very well have phoned from the Lodge, but that, too, was a matter of long established habit: business phone calls were not to be made through hotel switchboards. Paul Harper answered on the first ring. "Ross here, Pauley," Ross said. "Are you alone?"

"Yes, Mr. Ross."

"How is everything going?"

"Just fine, Mr. Ross."

Was there the echo of doubt in Harper's voice? "That anthropologist you mentioned," Ross said. "She is supporting the project?"

This time the hesitation was plain. "As a matter of fact," Harper said, "not at the moment. I expect to persuade her to come back, but—" Harper hesitated again.

"But what, Pauley?" Ross's voice was soft.

"She has a boy friend," Harper said. "He's a local cop, at least part Mex—"

"His name?"

"Ortiz. He's a lieutenant. He came around to see me."

"Why?"

"Look, Mr. Ross, everything's fine. It's just that at the moment things are a little confused. But I'll straighten them out. I'll—"

"I'm still waiting for information, Pauley."

"Yes, I know. I'll have that too. It's just that—"

"Pauley." There was the hint of sharpness in Ross's voice now. "I think you're trying not to tell me something. I don't like that. What are you not telling me?"

There was a long pause. Harper said at last, "There's a Treasury man named Snyder—"

"Tax man?"

"I thought so."

"And what does that mean?"

Hesitation was plain again; and reluctance. Harper said slowly, "According to the anthropologist he's a narcotics man, Mr. Ross. He had a report on Sly Investors, and he mentioned Midtown Enterprises. I told him to go through New York."

Ross was silent, thoughtful. He said at last, "I don't like it, Pauley. Why should a narcotics man have a report on Sly Investors?"

"I don't know, Mr. Ross."

Again the thoughtful silence. Then, "I think, Pauley," Ross said, "that you had better take a little trip. You've been working too hard. You're tired."

"I'm fine, Mr. Ross."

"I won't argue the point," Ross said. "Is that understood?"

A long pause. Then, "Yes, sir." There was resignation in Harper's voice.

"Keep in touch," Ross said. "I'll want to know where you are." Ross's voice altered subtly. "I think you and I are going to have to have a long talk, Pauley." He hung up and walked out of the booth and out into the plaza to sit down and think.

He sat for quite a while in the sun. The cathedral bells tolled the hour and Ross watched the tower pigeons take flight. Panic, he thought, was never the solution to anything. Somewhere there was always an answer, or at least an explanation. He stood up at last and crossed the plaza, walking steadily, heading for police headquarters. To the desk sergeant he said, "Lieutenant Ortiz, please. My name is Peter Ross." A solid citizen accustomed to dealing with public servants.

Johnny stood up when Ross walked in. "Sit down, Mr. Ross."

Ross sat down. So this was the man, he thought, and the warning bell tolled on. He said, "The last time I saw you, lieutenant, you were looking for a man named March. Did you find him?"

Johnny showed the white teeth. "You mean," he said, "does he exist? He does. I found him. My calling on you was purely accidental." He paused. "I assume your coming here is not."

A local cop at least part Mex, Harper had said, and the implication had been that Lieutenant Ortiz was not very much. So much for Harper's judgment, Ross thought; Lieutenant Ortiz was a long distance from being not very much. Tread warily, he told himself. "I'm a businessman, lieutenant," he said. "Raven Estates is one of my interests, and Paul Harper tells me that he has encountered a certain amount of harassment from your department."

Again the white teeth flashed. "Did he say that?" Johnny said. "Because we haven't started to harass him yet. I haven't even asked him questions."

"About what, lieutenant?"

Johnny thought about it. There were times for caution, and times for boldness, and he was inclined to think that this was a time to shoot the works. It could do very little harm that he could see, and it might very well stir up a fuss, which would be all to the good. "If you have a little time," he said, "I'll tell you a story, Mr. Ross."

Nothing showed in Ross's face. "I will take the time, lieutenant."

Johnny picked up a yellow sheet torn from the teletype machine. "This just came in," he said. "It shows that Paul Harper is an interesting fellow. He was a medico in the Army which is why his prints are on file. He lost his license to practice shortly after he came out of the Army, but his background of medicine explains several things." He paused. "Poisoning heroin in such a way that the poison would go unnoticed by the user and yet would be fatal probably isn't all that difficult, but a doctor would certainly know how to do it."

"I haven't any idea what you're talking about," Ross said. He smiled faintly. "I didn't know that Pauley was a doctor, but I don't see that it matters."

"Another thing a doctor would know," Johnny said as if Ross had not spoken, "is precisely where," he touched the back of his neck, "something sharp like an ice pick would kill a man instantly." He paused. "It did. No fuss, no muss, no bother."

"What man was that, lieutenant?"

"A man named Wilson." Johnny saw no sign of recognition in Ross's face; he had expected none; the man was good, very good. Johnny warmed to his story. "Walter Wilson," he said then, "who was wearing what I imagine to be a money belt which is missing, and a lightweight handgun in a hideaway holster, which is not missing."

Ross took his time. "I assume, lieutenant, that you

are speaking of the man found up on the ski slope?''
He watched Johnny nod. ''Why do you tell me this?''

''I'll let you decide.'' The small office was still.
''Aside from the missing belt,'' Johnny said, ''and the
handgun, and Wilson's luggage which is also gone,
there was something else Wilson had, but it was in the
motel safe. It was enough poisoned heroin for three
fixes. Wilson had been carrying it through Arizona and
Texas where in three different cities three men died of
poisoned heroin only a day or two after Harper had
been there ahead of him and had left town.''

''I still don't see,'' Ross said, ''what any of this has
to do with me, lieutenant.'' He paused. ''Or with Paul
Harper.''

''But,'' Johnny said, ''you aren't making any move
to leave, so, as I said, I'll let you decide why I'm telling
you the story. Okay?''

Outmaneuvered by a small-town cop, Ross told himself, and found the concept annoying. He allowed none
of the annoyance to show. ''I'll try to be patient,'' he
said.

''And I'll try to be brief.'' Johnny took a moment
or two to set his thoughts in order. ''In Tucson, Phoenix, and El Paso,'' he said, ''Harper and Wilson stayed
in the same motels only a few days apart.'' He raised
one hand in a silencing gesture. ''You don't know anything about this, Mr. Ross, so there's not much point
in your trying to refute my logic, now, is there?''

Ross made no answer. Along with the annoyance he
felt there was growing admiration, too, and he told
himself that he would do well to behave very carefully
where this man was concerned. ''Tell me, lieutenant,''

he said presently, "are you—I believe *chicano* is the word?"

Johnny could even smile, and mean it. "A red herring? But the answer is yes, partly. My father was part Anglo and part Spanish-American." Pause. "I think. My mother was Apache. I am me." His voice did not change. "So Harper and Ross stayed in the same motels and I find that interesting. What is even more interesting is that they both attended the local porno movie house here in Santo Cristo on the same day, the only time Harper ever went to it." He paused again. "The day Wilson was killed." A third pause. "He was killed, incidentally, Mr. Ross, in that porno movie house."

The office was again still. Tony Lopez appeared in the doorway. He looked at Ross and opened his mouth and then shut it again in silence. He looked at Johnny.

"Come in," Johnny said. "Sergeant Lopez, Mr. Ross. Lean against the wall and listen, Tony. I'm telling Mr. Ross a funny story."

Ross said, "All I can say, lieutenant, is that it is a strange, disconnected story, and I wonder if you are as sure as you sound of your facts."

"Quite sure," Johnny said. "Wilson was killed in the theatre. Somebody took his belt. Somebody also went to the motel where he was staying and took his luggage, but did not get the poisoned heroin in the motel safe."

Ross said quietly, "But I understood, lieutenant, that the dead man was found up on the ski slope. Was the newspaper account inaccurate?"

Again Tony Lopez opened his mouth, and again he

shut it carefully. It appeared to him that the Apache *brujo* had flipped his lid, but if there was one thing he was not going to do, it was make comment on the lapse.

"The newspaper account was accurate," Johnny said. "What happened was that someone found Wilson's body in the movie house and panicked." He shook his head. "No, it wasn't the murderer. We know who it was. It was snowing hard, and the man loaded Wilson's body into a snowmobile and took it up to the ski slope where it stayed the rest of the season under the snow." He paused. "You can believe that, Mr. Ross. We have the proof, and there's no point in my lying to you, anyway."

"Is that the end of the—fable, lieutenant?"

Tony, watching, expected anger, and was wrong again. Johnny was smiling. "Fables have conclusions, don't they, Mr. Ross? Let me give you mine. Somebody, for his own reasons, and I can guess what they were, poisoned some heroin and saw to it that one fix was sold in each of three cities. Wilson found out about it and somehow got some of the poisoned heroin as proof to take back to—" Johnny smiled again. "We think of it as the home office, Mr. Ross, the command post where someone sits and directs the drug traffic."

"Do you really believe that, lieutenant?"

Johnny nodded. "I do. But, then, I'm a simple fellow, and maybe I believe a lot of things that aren't true. Indulge me. Wilson wanted to take the poisoned heroin to the home office to show that somebody was deliberately lousing up the operation. But Wilson didn't get there. He got himself dead in the snow instead."

There was silence. Tony's ear began to itch, but he

decided against scratching it. He watched Ross steadily, and waited.

"You said," Ross said at last, "that you could guess at the reason why someone put poison in heroin. It seems to me a very strange thing to do."

"Does it?" Johnny said. "But I think the reason is fairly obvious." He smiled again. "And I'm sure if you bother to think about it, Mr. Ross, you'll come to the same conclusion I did. I'm also sure that the home office would come to the same conclusion—if they knew the facts." He pushed back his chair and stood up. "Thank you for coming in. It saved me another trip out to the Lodge."

Ross stood up slowly. "I admire your imagination, lieutenant." He seemed about to say more, and then changed his mind. "Good day," he said and walked out.

Tony Lopez still leaned against the wall, but now he was shaking his head in slow wonder. "Amigo, do you know what you have done?" But of course Johnny knew, Tony thought; Johnny had known right from the start. It was, Tony decided, just the kind of thing an Apache would think up. "You've stripped Harper naked and put him out in the desert without any water and just as sure as he's alive, he's dead. I almost feel sorry for him."

"Do you?" Johnny said. He was thinking of seven other dead men. "I don't."

18

Congressman Hawley was easy and affable in his greeting. "Come in, son," he told Snyder, the Treasury man. "This is Ben Hart, friend of mine." As Snyder and Ben shook hands, Hawley got out of his chair, went to the wall cupboard, and got out the bourbon bottle and three glasses. He poured them all, handed them around. "Ben," he said, "is real interested too in this Raven Estates business." He sat down then and smiled at Snyder.

The proper thing to do, of course, Snyder told himself, was to point out that his investigation was confidential, and he was sorry, but his lips were sealed. And he knew exactly where it would get him: nowhere. He didn't know a thing about Ben Hart except that he was a big local rancher, but Congressman Hawley was something else; and in Washington it was said and widely believed that if the old man was simply asking, a sensible man did well to answer before the congressman lost patience, stirred himself, and took action. Still Snyder hesitated.

"Have a taste of that bourbon," Mark Hawley said. "I'd appreciate your opinion of it." And then, without any change of inflection, "Of course, what we're asking for isn't confidential information. We wouldn't do that, now, would we, son?"

Snyder sipped the bourbon. It went down like fine wine. "Of course not, congressman," he said.

"Just the general outlines is all we're after."

"Yes, sir." Snyder held out his glass as the congressman raised the bottle. "Uh," he said, "I guess the best place to begin is at the beginning." He did.

The old men listened quietly, sipping their drinks, showing as much expression, Snyder thought, as you would expect to see around the table at a big-time poker game. As a matter of fact, he thought, what he was talking about was a big-time poker game, very big— the stakes, 16,000 acres valued at about $5,000,000. He hadn't thought of it that way before. The two old men probably had, but you wouldn't have known it from looking at them.

"Another touch of bourbon, son?" the congressman said and passed the bottle. "We do appreciate your coming here and filling us in. I think the Treasury has done a splendid job, and I'll see to it that you're given full marks." When the congressman smiled, he somehow resembled a crocodile in the shallows.

After Snyder was gone, Ben Hart said thoughtfully, "You kept track of all those companies and corporations?" He shook his head. "I got lost way back."

"I didn't even try to keep up," the congressman said. "Only two people are important: Harper and that fellow Ross, and I think maybe only Ross is real important.''

Ben thought about it. "Why, then," he said, "that makes things a lot simpler, doesn't it?"

The congressman helped himself to whiskey. He studied its color against the light from the windows. He said at last, "There's nothing fancy-footed about your thinking. There never was." He looked at Ben. "And maybe that's the best way, after all."

"There are ways and ways," Ben said. "Some places they gentle horses, one teensy little step at a time lest you hurt their feelings. I've always found the best way was to slap a saddle on and climb aboard and see who's the better man, you or the horse."

The congressman smiled that wicked smile. "Ever been thrown?"

"Why, hell yes. But the horse knew he'd had somebody on his back, and after I got myself picked up we went at it again. And again, if it had to be. Pretty soon the horse knows you aren't going to quit, so he does."

The congressman smiled once more. "As I said, maybe we don't need fancy-foot thinking."

Ross went from Johnny's office straight to that public telephone near the plaza. Again Harper answered on the first ring. "I've met Lieutenant Ortiz," Ross said without preamble, "and I think you and I had better have our little talk now, Pauley." He waited, but there was no response. "Did you hear me?" Ross said.

"Yes, sir."

"The lieutenant already knows that I am interested

in Raven Estates, so I'll come to your office." Pause. "Wait for me there."

"Yes, sir," Harper said. As he hung up, he thought: in a pig's eye. He had no idea how or why Ross and Ortiz had gotten together, but under the circumstances he didn't think it prudent to stay around and find out. It was, he decided, all the fault of that black anthropologist, who had gone straight to Ortiz with God only knew what kind of tales. And the more he thought about it, the madder he got.

Ross had not left the telephone booth. He put in another dime and dialed the operator. "This is a credit card call," he said, and gave his credit card number and the telephone number in New York. "I'll speak with anyone who answers." While he waited he thought again of Johnny Ortiz who was too damned smart to be a cop. Why, Ross thought, it was almost an affront to sensible men to have somebody of the lieutenant's caliber wasting himself that way.

A man's voice said, "Midtown Enterprises."

"This is Peter Ross, Bernie."

"Yes, sir."

"I'd like you to draw up a contract for me and hold it ready. It concerns Paul Harper of Raven Estates here in Santo Cristo."

There was no hesitation. "Yes, Mr. Ross."

"He's a very good man, Bernie, and if we sign the contract, we'll want him to be well taken care of."

"I'll see to it, Mr. Ross."

"I'll be staying here longer than I expected, Bernie, so I have another little chore for you." Ross paused for thought. As the lieutenant had said, there was no reason for him to lie, and the tale of the poisoned heroin had a good solid ring to it. "I've been told," Ross said, "that some damaged merchandise turned up late last year in Tucson, Phoenix, and El Paso. I want to know why I wasn't notified. I also want to know whether it was damaged in transit, or whether the shipment itself was at fault. We have a reputation to maintain, Bernie, and damaged or faulty merchandise does us no good at all." As the police lieutenant had seen just as clearly as he did, Ross thought, and again felt annoyance at the waste of talent. "Look into it for me, Bernie," Ross said.

"Will do, Mr. Ross."

Ross hung up, collected his dime, and walked out into the plaza again. He sat in the sun on the same bench he had occupied before while he thought about what he was going to say to Paul Harper. It did not even occur to him that Harper might run. There was no place for him to go.

A lot would depend, Ross thought, on Pauley's answers to a number of questions the lieutenant had raised; although, to be honest with himself, Ross also had to admit that his mind was pretty well made up, and the contract would be put through. He felt no pity, merely a sense of annoyance at the waste, because Pauley did have usefulness, or had had.

He felt too a further annoyance because obviously if Pauley had been misbehaving as the lieutenant indicated, he had not been doing it on his own. Pauley would not have dared to step that far out of line without someone behind him, and Ross could guess who that someone was—the fat toad of an ex-politician back in

Jersey who had always thought he was far more able than he was. An attempted take-over was just about his speed. But the ex-politician also enjoyed a kind of privileged position, and with it what amounted to immunity from frontal attack, and so in the end it would be Pauley who would pay the bill and thereby demonstrate that Peter Ross had not yet lost his touch, and was in no way prepared to relinquish his authority.

Ross sighed and got up from the sunny bench. He walked without haste across the plaza and down the street the short distance to the Raven Estates office. The front door was unlatched, and he walked inside. If there was a receptionist on the staff, she was out. So. That warning bell was tolling again.

Ross walked through into Harper's office. It was empty. Ross stood for a moment looking around, and then walked behind the desk and opened drawers. They were empty too. And all that was in the filing cabinet was an economy-size bottle of Tums. Pauley, Ross thought, would have done well to take the Tums with him. He was going to need them.

He sat down at the desk, picked up the phone, and placed his credit card call again. To the answering voice, "We will sign the contract, Bernie," he said.

"Very good, Mr. Ross."

"As soon as possible."

Ross hung up, and sat for a little time looking at the plat on the wall. Loose ends, he thought, but they could wait. Tomorrow he would find a dependable lawyer here in Santo Cristo to take over details and find out exactly where they stood. Obviously Paul Harper's reports were not to be believed at all. Pity.

As he stood up and walked out of the office, carefully closing the front door after him, he wondered if Cindy and her mother were at the Lodge pool. There might yet be time to join them. He still felt guilty about having let Cindy down.

Distances in Santo Cristo were not great. After all, the town had not been laid out originally, but had grown as it chose over the centuries, and during a large part of its history its residents had made their way from place to place either on foot or by horseback or carriage.

Harper left his car on a side street which had no parking meters where, with luck, it would remain without arousing attention for two or three days. He walked the rest of the way up Arroyo Road to the almost isolated house. There was no car in the carport, and, as nearly as he could tell, no one inside. The front door was locked. And the back door. But it was easy enough to force a small window in the rear of the house, and let himself in. He settled down at the telephone, pencil in hand, to spend the time profitably while he waited.

"I don't think," Tony Lopez said, "that Harper knows Sonny March. Sam Christopher says he doesn't, which doesn't mean much. My *primo*, Emilio, says he's never seen Harper near the March cottage, and that means a lot more." Tony paused. "And you already know that Harper knows Ross." Another pause. "Where does that get us?"

"I don't know," Johnny said. Simple truth.

"I've had a man asking questions about Pete Gardena, too," Tony said, "and that isn't getting us anywhere either. The only people who could testify that Pete actually sold that H are the ones who bought it, and they're all dead. Waldo Davega *says* he sold the stuff to Pete, but it's only his word against Pete's, and we don't have any actual proof that Waldo ever had the stuff in the beginning." Tony shrugged his wide shoulders. "We are wandering around, amigo, like a dude lost in the mountains." Pause. *"Verdad?"*

True enough, and Johnny was prepared to admit it. "You find bear tracks," he said. "You may never find the bear, but you can see that here he turned over a rock and there he found some wild honey and in a third place he ate some berries." Johnny shrugged. "You may not be able to say what color he is, but you know his size, and how he moves—"

Tony said, *"You* know, amigo, not me." He had seen Johnny tracking, and he still didn't believe it, but there it was. "So now we're hunting bear?"

Johnny smiled. "Like I said, you may never find the bear no matter how much you know about him." He paused. "On the other hand, you may come around a turn in the trail and catch him by surprise, and get to know him awful fast a lot better than you figured to."

Tony thought about it. At last he said, "You are saying, no, that the next move is up to the bear?"

Johnny nodded. "Something like that. Unless somebody does something, all we have is theory." He pushed back his chair and stood up. "I think we call it a day." Admission, he told himself, of defeat.

Outside the sun was bright and the sky blue and the air dry and brisk. There were the mountains, untroubled, ageless. And here I am, Johnny thought, moping; which was a ridiculous state of affairs, but not at the moment capable of change.

You won some and you lost some—it was a practical working philosophy, Johnny supposed, for ballplayers and yachtsmen and maybe even lawyers. But it sure as hell didn't satisfy him. That a worthless character like Pete Gardena was beyond his reach galled him. That Peter Ross who, he was now convinced, was well up in the hierarchy of an organization devoted among other things to heroin distribution and sales was even free to walk around, let alone visit openly and in luxury at the Lodge, brought on cold anger. That Paul Harper might be disciplined or even liquidated by Peter Ross's command brought no sense of satisfaction because there ought to have been a legal way to lower the boom on Harper; and maybe there had been at that, and Johnny just hadn't been able to see it—bitter thought.

It was rare, this what-ever-made-me-think-I-was-a-good-cop-anyway feeling, but he had it now. Maybe in trying to deal with people like Ross and Harper he was out of his league. Or maybe, as Cassie had suggested, he had built up too much theory on too little fact and the result was a top-heavy structure of mere suspicion that could fall over and come apart like Humpty Dumpty. Maybe, maybe, maybe.

He walked to his pick-up and got in. In his present mood, he thought, he wasn't really fit company for man or beast, and not too long ago he would have gone off in solitude to nurse his grudge and taste its bile. It was a measure of change in him that was almost transformation that there was no smallest doubt where he was going when he switched on the engine and put the truck in gear. Cassie would be home from the museum by now, and he headed for her house up on Arroyo Road as to sanctuary.

Cassie's car was in the carport. Johnny parked behind it, got out, and walked to the front door. He had his hand raised to knock when the door opened and Cassie stared at him as if she were seeing a ghost.

"Chica," Johnny's voice was filled with concern, "what's wrong?"

She shook her head in silence. Her eyes seemed to be telling him something, but he had no idea what.

"Are you going to let me in?" Johnny said.

Cassie closed her eyes in defeat. She opened them slowly and shook her head apologetically. Then she stepped back and Johnny walked inside. There he stopped.

It was Harper who closed the door. He had a handgun pointed at Johnny's stomach, and it was evident from the way he held it that it was not the first time he had been in this position. "Slow and easy," Harper said. "Just turn around."

Johnny turned. He felt Harper's hand frisking him. He endured.

"I guess you're clean," Harper said. "You can go over there and sit down on the sofa. You, too, Cassie."

They sat close together, but not touching. "I'm sorry, Johnny," Cassie said. "He was here when I got home. He—" She shook her head in near-disbelief.

"Where's Chico?" Johnny said.

Cassie closed her eyes. She said nothing.

Harper said, "He tried to bite me. I don't take that.

He won't try to bite anybody else.'' He sat down in an easy chair and rested the gun lightly on his knee.

Johnny said slowly, "You and I—" He left it there. "Never mind. Just what do you think you're trying to accomplish by this?"

It was Cassie who answered. Her voice was not steady. "The airport, Johnny." She caught her lower lip between her teeth, and for a moment there were no more words. Then, "He's going to hijack a plane. Like those three men at Albuquerque." Her voice was rising.

"Easy, chica, easy."

"And," Harper said, "you're going to help me. Between the two of you, you got me into this. You're going to get me out." He consulted a piece of paper covered with his own handwriting. "There's a westbound flight coming in from New York, Chicago, and Oklahoma City at nineteen hundred. It's on the ground in Santo Cristo for only twenty minutes, then it goes on to Phoenix and Los Angeles." He shook his head. "You're wrong in what you're thinking, Cassie." He smiled faintly. "You've lost your scientific objectivity. I don't intend to hijack the plane, unless I have to. I just want to be sure I get aboard." He gestured with the gun at Johnny. "That's where you come in. You get me aboard."

Cassie started to speak. Johnny laid his hand on her arm. "It makes no sense," he said to Harper.

"It does to me."

"Until now," Johnny said, "we weren't doing any more than looking into your activities. We wouldn't have stopped you from boarding an airplane."

"Maybe."

"So now we have it out in the open," Johnny said. He reached for Cassie's hand and held it tight. His eyes did not leave Harper's face. "You aren't running from us, the police; you're running from Ross, no?"

"What did you tell him?" Harper's voice was unnatural now, tight, angry.

"Didn't he say?"

Harper's headshake was almost, but not quite, imperceptible. "I didn't wait to find out. All it takes is a phone call from him—" He stopped. "Goddam you, anyway. If you hadn't mixed in—"

"You've got it wrong," Johnny said. The anger he felt was banked, controlled, a steady force. He still held Cassie's hand tightly. "You tried playing both ends against the middle, doctor, and that's a tough act."

Cassie said slowly, wonderingly, "Doctor?"

"MD," Johnny said, "defrocked, for cause." With his free hand he made a small gesture of dismissal. "Unimportant, except that it's just one more thing pointing a direction." Then, to Harper again, "Your connection with poisoned dope wasn't supposed to be known. But everything went wrong, didn't it? Wilson found out about it. How?"

Harper took his time. "You're making up the story," he said at last.

"All right," Johnny said, "maybe we'll never know how Wilson found out. Probably somebody told him what was going on. It doesn't make any difference now. He didn't catch up with you until he got here to Santo Cristo, and probably he asked you if you'd heard any word about poisoned heroin. After all, you worked for the same firm, the same boss, why wouldn't he ask you?''

"This," Harper said, "is what you told Mr. Ross?"

"Part of it. The rest is about the murder in the porno theatre by pithing—something a doctor would know about. And about the missing belt, probably a money belt. And about the bad H that was in the motel safe. And about the man who panicked and loaded Wilson's body on a snowmobile and took it up to the ski slope.'' Johnny paused. "That must have been a shock. When the body didn't turn up, I mean."

Harper said slowly, carefully, "Do you know what I ought to do? I ought to shoot you right now, in the belly where it would take you a long time to die."

"Your version of staking someone out on an ant hill," Johnny said. He nodded. "But then you might not get aboard that plane." He paused. "And you're sure Ross has already made his phone call, and your name is on the list, and without me you can't even be sure you'd get to the airport, let alone off to Phoenix and LA."

There was silence. Johnny squeezed Cassie's hand once more. The bear had made the next move, as Tony Lopez had thought, Johnny told himself; and liked it not. He wondered how carefully Harper had thought it through, because there was an obvious fallacy in his plan as stated, and Johnny had to know whether he saw it. "Suppose I get you aboard that plane," he said. "What then?"

"You don't see me again," Harper said.

"You have money?" Johnny nodded and answered his own question. "What was in the money belt was probably enough to last for quite a while." Then the big question: "What's to prevent me from radioing ahead to Phoenix that you're aboard and we want you held? You're going to shoot me in the airport in front of a lot of people just to keep me quiet?"

Harper shook his head. He seemed calmer now, the anger he had allowed to show pushed back into its cage. "I won't do any shooting unless I have to. What will keep you from doing anything foolish is Cassie. She'll be on that airplane with me, and if anybody stops me at Phoenix or LA, wherever I decide to get off, your high-yellow girl is dead."

19

Trans-National Airlines Flight #118, westbound from La Guardia to Los Angeles International, carried only six passengers in first-class when it took off from its Oklahoma City stop; in stewardess parlance: two doubles and two singles.

One of the doubles was a pretty young woman and an older man, screen hopeful with agent. "X-rated?" one stewardess wondered.

The other stewardess shook her head. "She isn't big enough here," she touched her own considerable bosom lightly, "for nude scenes."

The two singles were widely separated businessmen, one of whom had littered his adjoining seat with papers and charts before they even took off from La Guardia; and the other, coming aboard at the O'Hare stop, promptly did the same.

The second double was two men. They were in their early thirties, quietly, even conservatively dressed in muted tweed jackets and dark flannel trousers. They smiled but did not speak to the stewardesses when they came aboard at La Guardia, asked for a table as soon as they were airborne, and settled down to gin rummy. When dinner was served, they accepted neither cocktail nor wine. They talked little over the meal, and with coffee returned to gin rummy.

"TV producers or directors, maybe?" the first stewardess said. "You get some weird ones."

The other stewardess thought not. "They aren't going on to LA; they're getting off at Santo Cristo. Anyway, TV types tend to chatter. And these don't even drink—how about that?"

The first stewardess lifted her shoulders and let them fall. "We get all kinds," she said. "Maybe these are what my father used to call bible-bangers."

The other stewardess smiled. "Playing gin?"

"Time to go," Harper said, and gestured lightly with the gun. "Just remember," he said to Johnny, "the first shot I have to fire goes to her."

Johnny's rifle was in the rack across the rear window of the pick-up. "I'll take that," Harper said, and did. He walked a few steps away from the truck, worked the rifle's bolt, and ejected five cartridges. He picked the cartridges up and carried them back to put in the glove compartment. "Just so you'll have a little time to think before you try anything," he said to Johnny. "Let's go."

Johnny drove; Cassie sat between the two men. Harper's tension seemed to have disappeared. "In some ways," he said, "I'm sorry to be leaving Santo Cristo. Nice town."

"We like it," Johnny said. He was conscious that

Cassie was watching him, probably waiting for him to produce a miracle, take the gun away from Harper without a shot being fired. Well, it wasn't going to happen that way. Harper was a pro; that stuck out. And with what was already hanging over him, he had nothing more to lose, which made him a dangerous pro, not to be taken lightly. No, Johnny thought, if he and Cassie were going to get out of this at all, it would only be by playing it cool and hoping for some kind of break. "Maybe," he said, "that's why we don't want people like you coming in and lousing our country up."

"Now, that's no way to talk," Harper said. "We were going to bring you the benefits of civilization." He smiled at Cassie. "All the lovely benefits you predicted: overcrowding, pollution, unemployment, lack of water—"

"Stop it!" Cassie said.

"Easy, chica." This was Johnny.

Harper said, "As an anthropologist, doctor, you ought to be interested in human behavior, and not immediately critical of it. Here I am—"

"Running scared," Johnny said.

Harper was briefly silent. Then he nodded. "I admit it. Medically speaking, it is a good way to run. Fear produces adrenalin, and adrenalin helps."

Cassie's eyes were closed. It seemed to her that both men were displaying a kind of little-boy bravado, and she wished they would stop. The situation was unreal, and terrifying. If I do get on that plane with him, she thought, what then? He is bitter; he has to be bitter; he even showed it when he called me a high-yellow girl. What happens then, when we get off the plane into darkness in a strange place? How will the bitterness come out? She tried to stop the questions, but they would not be stilled.

Johnny said, "What I want to know is where do you figure to drop out of sight? From what I hear the syndicate, organization, whatever you want to call it has people in just about every hole you might try to hide in, no?"

"My business," Harper said.

"Of course," Johnny said, "I don't know for sure. I can only guess. But if I were running things as Ross does, then I'd think pretty much the way the Postal Service people do. They'll spend whatever money and time it takes to run down any mail theft, which is why mail boxes out on country roads are as safe as they are. If Ross let you get away with your performance, he would just be encouraging others, *verdad?* And so—"

"And so," Harper said, and his voice was no longer easy, "you'll shut up. Turn here, into the parking lot. So. We'll walk to the airport building. Cassie can carry the bag; it isn't heavy and it goes aboard with us. Here." He held out two bills to Johnny. "Two hundred dollars. You buy the tickets. The reservations are in the name of Hawkins, two one-way tickets to LA."

Cassie stood a little way from the ticket counter with Harper. He had a light raincoat folded over his left arm, his right hand crossed beneath it. "Look pleasant," he said. He was smiling. "Think happy thoughts, doctor, and maybe you'll get back to your Arroyo Road dig yet. Maybe."

Cassie was suddenly, not calm, but resigned. "There are words for people like you," she said.

"Temper, temper." Harper was watching Johnny at the counter. "An intelligent man," he said. "You see?" Johnny had turned away from the counter, and was gesturing with the ticket envelope he held toward the escalator. "Let's go," Harper said.

They rode the escalator up, crossed the upper lobby, and rode another escalator down, walked the long corridor beneath the runway, and rode up again to the surface. Overhead the loudspeaker said, "Trans-National Airlines Flight number one eighteen, from Oklahoma City, Chicago, and New York, now arriving at Gate Four. Passengers for Phoenix and Los Angeles will please prepare to board."

"Nice timing," Harper said. He sounded pleased with himself.

Through the windows of the building they could see the lights of the field, and the taxiing jet following the arm signals of the man on the ground as it swung slowly into position by the gate. The jet engines died. The self-propelled stairs drove up and the doors of the plane opened.

"I'll check us in," Johnny said. He started for the check-in desk.

Harper said, "Us?" His voice was cold.

"I'm going with you," Johnny said. "You didn't think you were going alone, did you?" He held up the envelope. "Three tickets." He was facing Harper squarely, waiting. Confrontation.

Passengers were already coming down the stairs from the plane, the two gin rummy players from the first-class compartment in the lead. They crossed the few yards to the building, opened the door, and walked inside.

Harper said to Johnny, "You're making it hard on yourself. And on her. You're trying to bluff—" He stopped, and his mouth opened involuntarily, and for a moment there was total silence.

Then, "Why, hello, Pauley," one of the men from the airplane said. He was smiling. It was not a pleasant smile. "Going somewhere?"

Harper lunged forward between the two men and crowded through those behind them. He ran for the door to the field and through it, and turned immediately out of the glare of the field lights. The last they saw of him was a flash of the light raincoat disappearing into the darkness.

If Johnny had not caught her arm, Cassie would have fallen.

"And so," Johnny said, "instead of the cavalry, the bad guys arrived in the nick of time. But the result was the same." It was morning and he was sitting at his desk talking to Tony Lopez, not feeling as unconcerned as he sounded. "We have an APB out on Harper. We can charge him with kidnaping, if nothing else. If and when we find him." He paused. "And if he's still alive."

"How about the baddies?" Tony said. His tone was eager.

Johnny smiled without amusement. "They're businessmen from New York. They work for an outfit called Midtown Enterprises. Friends of Harper's, they said, and they can't imagine why he panicked."

"Weapons?"

Johnny smiled again. "Not on them. Nothing as crude as that. They're hunters, they say. They have gun cases in their luggage. They also have fishing gear." The smile disappeared. "If we started shaking down everybody who came into the state with guns and fishing tackle, can you imagine what would happen?"

Tony could well imagine what would happen: from the governor down, the entire state apparatus would shudder and writhe because the state's main industry was tourism, and among its principal attractions were some of the finest hunting and fishing in the country. Tony's sense of impotence was both deep and bitter.

"We'll keep an eye on them," Johnny said, "but not close enough to give them cause for complaint."

Tony swore softly in Spanish. In English he said, "Yes, sir, please, sir, kiss your ass, sir. No, not you, amigo, them. Do I tip my hat to them? And to Ross, if I see him?"

Johnny knew exactly how he felt. "We can't even touch Pete Gardena," he said. His voice was mild, but the anger he felt was difficult to control. "Harper is the one I want," he said. "Then we'll see about the others."

He and Cassie had buried Chico that morning in a grave Johnny had dug and lined with bricks against marauding wildlife. Cassie wept. "He didn't have to—kill him."

"Chica." Johnny's voice was quiet. "To men like Harper, whatever gets in the way is no more important than a fly to be squashed. We'll find another Chico."

"I don't want another. Not ever."

206

"You're backsliding into isolation," Johnny said. One more thing for Harper to atone for.

Johnny had another chore to attend to before he left Cassie's house that morning. He spent some time hunkered down studying the ground near the spot where the pick-up had been parked last night. There were Harper's footprints plain in the dirt where he had walked off, carrying Johnny's rifle, three, four steps, enough to show how he walked—enough to identify him to Johnny's eyes for all time.

Cassie watched in silence, and shivered faintly. When Johnny rose and automatically brushed the knees of his trousers, his face was expressionless, but his voice held conviction. "We'll find him, chica."

"Johnny—" Cassie stopped and shook her head.

"And then," Johnny said, "he won't go around killing anything else."

Now, in his office, facing facts rather than emotions, he was not so sure. "He has a lot of room," he said to Tony, "a hundred and twenty-one thousand six hundred and sixty-six square miles, to be precise, without even going out of state. Where would he run?"

Tony lifted the wide shoulders and let them fall.

"He's a big-city boy," Johnny said, "with, I think, big-city instincts."

"This isn't a big city, amigo."

True. Johnny thought about it. Dropping out of sight in Santo Cristo would be not at all like dropping out of sight in, say, New York, or LA; hidey holes were too few and too far between. Out in the country was another matter. "I've heard that he's a skier," he said. He was merely groping, searching for a handle.

Tony shook his head. "You have to walk up awful big mountains to find enough snow for skiing this time of year. Besides—" He spread his hands. "A dead end. There's no place to go once you've walked up."

Also true. Johnny was silent, thoughtful.

"The part of the country he does know," Tony said, "is Raven Estates—and where does that get us?" He spread his hands again. "Jackrabbits, horny toads, a rattlesnake or two, and only piñon and juniper and chamisa to hide in—not even any buildings." He stopped and studied Johnny's face. "What have I said now?"

"Buildings," Johnny said. "It's buildings a city boy thinks of, isn't it?"

Tony had no idea where agreement might lead him. He nodded warily.

"Where are the nearest buildings to Raven Estates?"

Tony thought about it. "The only place anywhere near," he said, "is Ben Hart's ranch." His face lightened. "You think?"

"He doesn't have much money," Johnny said. "Cassie was carrying the suitcase, and there was ninety thousand dollars in it."

Tony whistled softly.

"How much of it," Johnny said, "he got from that money belt we think Wilson was wearing, there's no way of knowing. But our best guess is that wherever it came from, it was Harper's getaway money, and now he's stranded without it." He paused and studied Tony. "You have a handgun," he said, "and the clothes you're wearing, and probably no friends you can trust. What would you do?"

Tony shook his head.

"He'd have to figure," Johnny said, "that the first thing I'd do would be to put out a wanted on him. That means the airport, the bus terminal, probably even the highways are all off-limits, no?"

Tony knew the technique: in tracking man or beast the thing to do was to try to put yourself in the quarry's skin and see the world as he saw it; then, and only then, you might be able to anticipate his next move. Like the boy hunting the lost cow: "I asked myself where I'd be if I was a cow, and I went there and she was." The only thing was, some were better at it than others. "So what do you think he'd do, amigo?" Wrong question. "What would you do in his place?"

"I think," Johnny said slowly, "that I'd figure to hole up until the fuzz relaxed a little. You can't keep roadblocks up forever, and after two, three days without any trace of the man you're after, you tend to think that somehow he slipped through, and the place to look for him is maybe somewhere else."

Perfectly obvious when it was spelled out for you. Tony nodded.

"He started from the airport," Johnny said. "There's nothing beyond it except open country, and if he went that way on foot—"

"The buzzards will show us where he got to," Tony said. It was a pleasant thought, he decided, although also entirely too far-fetched.

"But from the airport," Johnny said, "on foot, there are several places that aren't out of reach." His thoughts were running smoothly now; he *was* Harper, alone and scared, but also thinking hard. "It's dark," he said, "and he's wearing city clothes, city shoes—"

"He's in for a rough time," Tony said. "Patches of prickly pear, and cholla, and running into those in the dark—" He shook his head. "That cactus can skin you alive."

True enough. Johnny smiled at the concept. "But as he said last night, he's got adrenalin flowing, and he knows if I catch him he's in for a bad time, and if the others catch him, he's dead." He was silent, examining his reasoning and finding no flaws. "So he does the best he can, because he's got to find a hiding place before sunup."

"And," Tony said, "your guess is Ben Hart's ranch buildings?"

"That's just a guess," Johnny said. "There are other possibilities. We'll start at the airport."

Tony opened his mouth to object, and then closed it again in silence. No use, he thought. If the Indian's mind was made up—

"I know his tracks," Johnny said. "Once he's off the runway and the blacktop and on the dirt, if he went cross-country, we'll find him."

No doubts, Tony thought, none. And the unbelievable part of it was that what the man said was no more than simple truth: if Harper had gone cross-country from the airport, he was as good as caught, period.

"First, though," Johnny said, "we'll tell Ben to be on the lookout." He got out of his chair. "On our way."

20

They drove Johnny's pick-up, Johnny's rifle, re-loaded, secure in the rack across the cab window. They jounced in over the cattle guard at the entrance to Ben's ranch, and raised a plume of dust the eight miles to the main ranch house. A familiar car was parked out front.

"Mark Hawley," Johnny said, and felt a measure of satisfaction that the congressman was on the ground. "Funny. For years he and Ben were like a couple of bull elk in rut; every time they ran into each other there was trouble. Now they're pals again." Because of Cassie, he thought; many changes had occurred because of Cassie, the changes in himself included. Harper hadn't known it, but by picking on Cassie he had stuck his finger in a lot of eyes in and around Santo Cristo.

They gathered in the great two-storied living room, Mark Hawley in a deep chair, Ben Hart standing by the fireplace while Johnny talked about last night. Tony leaned against the wall, watching and listening in silence. The two old men were throwbacks to the bare-knuckle days, he thought, and he could pretty well anticipate their reactions. He was right.

Ben Hart said, "You think he might be on the ranch here somewhere." It was a statement, no question. He nodded, left the fireplace, and crossed the broad room. He took a key out of his vest pocket and unlocked the gun cabinet, took out a rifle, hesitated, turned, and looked at the congressman. "You want one too?"

"Why, hell yes," the congressman said, "you think I've forgotten how to shoot one?" He heaved himself out of his chair.

Tony, still leaning against the wall, tried not to smile.

Johnny said, "He may not be here."

"Of course not," Ben Hart said. "But if he is, we'll pick him up for you." He handed a rifle to Hawley. "Either way," he said, "after we're done here, I think we'll go attend to another little chore."

"It's about time," the congressman said.

Tony frowned in puzzlement. Johnny looked as if he had heard nothing. "We'll be on our way," he said. He smiled. "Good hunting."

Back out the long dusty road to the highway, then south past Raven Estates to the airport. Johnny parked the pick-up and they went inside to talk with the airport manager.

"Help yourself," the manager said. "You've got a lot of fence to ride," he shrugged, "but if you think it's worthwhile."

"It is," Johnny said.

"Just don't clutter the runways."

Johnny and Tony walked, as Johnny had walked last night with Harper and Cassie, the length of the long corridor beneath the main runway, and took the escalator to the building at ground level. There they walked outside through the door Harper had taken in his flight. Johnny looked around.

"He went that way, into the dark."

"But that's back toward the main building," Tony said, "lights, people, the road back to town—" He shook his head. "No way."

"Right," Johnny said. He pointed in the opposite direction. "Even if he doubled back and went out that way, over the fence or through a gate somewhere—"

"He's got sixty miles to go on foot without water," Tony said, "and we don't have to worry about him any more." If he had gone that way, maybe one day, Tony thought, somebody on horseback or cutting across country in a jeep might find what was left of Harper. Maybe; there was an awful lot of country there.

"If he went that way," Johnny said, pointing, "then he's headed for Ben's ranch, and we can leave that to Ben and Mark Hawley."

Tony was frowning now. "That leaves what?" He was staring at the mountains in the fourth quadrant. "There's nothing in there except some old mine workings."

"And Granada," Johnny said. "Never been there?"

"I," Tony said, "will be damned. Sure I've been there. As a kid." He shook his head in wonderment. "And it's been written up, that woman who goes around taking pictures of ghost towns—"

"And maybe," Johnny said, "just maybe, Harper read about it." He turned back to the building. "We'll check outside the fence in that direction."

He even made it look easy, Tony thought; that was the part that galled you.

Sometime during the night a wind had come up, but Harper, sleeping the drugged sleep of exhaustion, did not hear it. Now, awake at last, aching and sore, he listened to its banshee wail as it blew through glassless windows and open doorways, rattled broken shutters, and set loose corrugated roofs to clanging. As he looked out at the empty street a tumbleweed came romping past touching the ground only at long intervals like a jackrabbit with a coyote not far behind.

When Harper stood up one foot felt awkward and he glared down at a two-inch piece of cholla cactus still clinging to the edge of his sole. He rubbed it off against the door frame with a savage, angry movement. This goddamned country ought to have been left to the Indians, he thought; they deserved it. And that, of course, brought Johnny Ortiz to mind, and now Harper's anger had its focus.

Wilson to Cassie to Ortiz; it sounded almost like a double-play combination—Tinker to Evers to Chance. And that was precisely the way his bad luck had run.

First, Wilson somehow getting on to the fact of cyanided heroin, and prepared to carry some of it back to New York as proof that somebody was making trouble. Okay, scratch Wilson, and it ought to have ended right there: a man wearing a gun, dead in a porno movie house—how deep would the fuzz have dug into what was obviously a killing in what the papers liked to call gangland?

But, no. Somehow the goddamned body disappeared

and didn't turn up for three months, and then, of course, it was a mystery no one could resist poking into.

Then that Cassie Enright chick with her local reputation, almost like a voodoo witch, believed by everybody in whatever she said that had anything even vaguely to do with anthropology, the science of man, and who better to be connected with the land development? And once Harper had mentioned her to Ross, he had to have her, there was no other way. So here came Johnny Ortiz because where the high-yellow bitch went, the Indian was right behind.

Harper ought to have taken care of Ortiz last night before he even left Cassie's house. Nobody had been watching the airport that he could see, and the girl alone would have been guarantee enough. Of course, Willie and Lew would still have come through the doorway as they had, and he would have known what that meant; but, still, in some obscure way the whole mess was at least partly Johnny Ortiz's fault. And the hell of it was that he, Harper, wasn't going to be able to pay Ortiz back for the trouble he had caused, because the one thing Harper had to do was drop completely out of sight or he was dead.

Another tumbleweed romped past and disappeared down the hill. Harper stared after it. It was hard to believe that people had ever actually lived here, he thought, just as it was hard to believe that people had ever lived in those caves called cliff-dwellings; but enough of his scientific training remained to convince him that it was so.

People had lived here when the mines were producing and maybe their ghosts still whispered in the empty buildings. Harper did not believe in ghosts, but it was a thought to toy with anyway. He needed something to think about, because, God knew, it was going to be a long two or three days before he dared to venture down to the airport again where in the big parking area he was pretty sure he could find a car with the keys still in it. Right now, he would be willing to bet, the place was swarming with fuzz.

But they would give up after a while. He had only to wait. He had no food, but without exertion in mild weather a man could last a long time without food, so he had no worry there. And there was that little trickle of a stream coming out of the mountain, so water was no problem either.

He was stiff and sore, but that would pass. Some of the deep scratches like claw marks on his legs could cause trouble, but there was nothing he could do about them, so that was that. He had an idea that for a long time he was going to dream about those patches of cactus into which he had blundered in the dark, and he wouldn't be surprised if sometimes he awakened screaming. He had read once that Apaches liked to strip their victims naked, toss them into great beds of cactus, and watch them try to fight their way out. Hilarious fun. Right back to Johnny Ortiz, who would probably enjoy the spectacle too.

Harper told himself to forget Johnny Ortiz. And Cassie Enright. And, for that matter, Walt Wilson, too. Brooding could only lead to helpless rage, and that was the worst thing a man alone and hungry and still on edge from fear could possibly work himself into. Count your blessings, Harper.

All right. He was alive; that was the paramount thing. He was alive and he was free, and not even seriously injured. He had his gun. He had lost his money, but already he was reconciled to that; somehow in these surroundings money lost much of its importance. He would get more. He had only to wait a few days and then venture back into civilization.

The wind howled, and he wished it would stop, but that too he could endure. Here in this ghost town he had read about and one day out of curiosity had visited, he was safe. In that fact was comfort.

It was while that thought was still in his mind that he saw the pick-up truck come over the brow of the hill and stop. Johnny Ortiz got out. He had a rifle in his hand.

Tony stepped out of the truck on his side. He too carried a rifle; and a handgun in his belt holster. He stood for a moment looking around at the sagging buildings, the empty windows like eye sockets in a skull; feeling the sense of desolation and waste as if the wilderness had moved in to reclaim its own. The wind howled in the narrow street raising a cloud of fine, gritty dust. "Just the way I remember it," Tony said. "A homey place, no?" He was being facetious, of course; and yet, he thought, to a man on the run this could look like a haven, sanctuary. Until we show up, he thought. He knew now in his bones that Johnny had had it right again.

Johnny, rifle in hand, was swinging a circle on the dirt of the street, his eyes searching the ground. Wind had done much to dissipate any tracks there might be, but at least there had not been rain to wipe away all traces, and maybe—yes, there, and there . . . and there; stooping, he followed the faint outlines of a man's footprints, a man close to exhaustion, a man with a piece of cactus caught on the edge of his sole making scratch marks in the dirt at every stride, a man named Harper.

Johnny straightened then and studied the row of frame houses that lined the street. You pay your money, he thought, and you take your choice. So be it. He lifted his voice: "Harper! Harper! We know you're here! Come out, or I'll come in after you!"

It smacked of magic, Harper thought, and that concept alone was enough to loosen the strings that held a man's confidence taut. He had watched Johnny swinging his circle, almost seeming to sniff as a hound would sniff at a trail; and although Harper had heard of such things, he had not really believed that there were trackers who could read sign as readily as a commuter read his morning paper.

But even accepting that there were such men, and Ortiz was one, how had he come here to this place of all places? That was the question that echoed fearfully in his mind. He had no idea that in the darkness he had left a cross-country trail clear as a highway but far more crooked; lurching here and there, stumbling over rocks, thrashing through cactus patches, blundering into piñon and juniper, climbing the hill at last to sanctuary. Johnny had needed to stop the pick-up only three times on the way to check on foot that his guess of destination was right.

"Harper!" Johnny's voice raised again. "Ten seconds! No more!" He was watching the houses carefully, but he saw nothing resembling a man, and he guessed that wherever Harper was he was standing motionless well back in shadow. Give Harper good marks for concealment.

Tony said softly, "Amigo. House by house?" It was the hard, bitter way to clear an area, but how else?

"You take the back of the row," Johnny said. "You'll have a clear view if he comes out. I'll take the front." He raised his voice again. "Time's up, Harper!" Stooping, the rifle at the ready, he began to run, zigzagging, toward the nearest house.

Never mind how he got here, Harper told himself; there he is. He watched the other, taller one, move out of sight, and he guessed correctly that he was covering the rear. That left what the football announcers loved to call a one-on-one situation. Better, much better. His confidence was beginning to steady itself. He moved cautiously in the shadows and strained for a look at Johnny, closer now, dodging still, and then, quickly, straightening in a rush and disappearing behind the structure of the house itself.

Steady, Harper told himself; make him come to you, and then the handgun against the rifle will give you the advantage. Comforting thought. There was, after all, nothing supernatural about the pick-up's appearance. They could have searched every other possibility first. Or it could have been pure blind guesswork. The point was that he, Harper, an educated man, a white man, was up against a couple of small-town cops, and there ought to be no doubt about the outcome. Never mind what he should have done before. Never mind anything but the here and now. He crouched, waiting, his eyes fixed on the gaping front doorway through which Johnny was bound to come.

He heard a sound on the front porch that had to mean footsteps. He moved forward a single step, remaining still in the shadows. The sound of the footstep was not repeated, and it occurred to Harper too late that there ought to have been a shadow cast by a man on the porch. And that meant—

"Right here," Johnny's voice said.

Harper turned quickly. The rifle was pointing at him through the side window. Its barrel did not move, and Johnny's angry, Indian eyes, watched the man inside almost in hope.

Harper ran. Crouching, rushing, through the empty front doorway, off the porch, into the street and away, toward the distant end of the row of houses.

Johnny came around the corner of the house at a trot. He stopped when he saw the running man, and he took his time, setting his feet, swinging the rifle smoothly to his shoulder, catching the target full in his sights. Like shooting fish in a rain barrel—and where did that sudden thought come from? And why? He steadied the sights on the broad of Harper's back, and his hand tightened around trigger and pistol grip. A nice clean kill, settling matters once and for all—why, then, the hesitation?

He knew the answer. It was one word: Cassie. His hand was still tightening as he lowered the muzzle of the rifle and steadied the sights on the running legs. The single shot echoed in the row of empty houses. The running man went down on his face in the dirt in a long slide. He screamed, and the gun flew from his hand, well out of reach. Johnny walked forward, the rifle at the ready. There was no need for a second shot.

Tony trotted up. He looked down at Harper who was sitting now, twisting the leg of his trousers into a makeshift tourniquet. "Bad shot, amigo," Tony said. "You had him—" He shrugged.

Johnny nodded. "Bad shot," he said, and that was all.

There were lights in Cassie's house. Johnny parked the pick-up behind Cassie's car and walked up to the door. He knocked and waited, and the door opened and there she was. "May we come in?" Johnny said.

"We?" The smooth brown face was puzzled.

Johnny raised his hands. He held a puppy, round and fuzzy with a pink tongue that protruded unbelievably, and a black-tipped tail that waved. "We," Johnny said, and watched the hesitation in Cassie's face, tension growing.

And then, all at once, the hesitation disappeared, and the tension, and it was as if a light had been turned on behind her eyes. She nodded and stepped back. "Welcome," she said. "Both of you." She was close to tears, and smiling, and how could that be? "Always," she said.

POSTSCRIPT

Sonny and Betty March waved Johnny to a halt on the plaza. "A party," Betty said. "And you're invited, lieutenant, you and that delightful Dr. Enright." Betty took a deep breath that brought her bosom to full splendor. "I'm that happy," she said, "I am indeed. That horrid man Ross is gone and we're back in Cottage A, where we've always stayed—"

"I told you it would only be for a few days," Sonny said. He seemed relieved.

"No thanks to you," Betty said. "I don't know what Congressman Hawley and Ben Hart said to that Ross man, but they left that very afternoon, he and his wife and daughter and two guests. Men." Betty smiled. "They were rather cute, at that."

"I see," Johnny said.

And because he liked matters made plain, he stopped around at Mark Hawley's office and accepted a drink of the congressman's fine bourbon. "Well," Mark Hawley said, "you know how things tend to happen sometimes, son. It was just a friendly visit Ben and I paid on Ross, but maybe he misunderstood." The old man smiled his crocodile-in-the-shallows smile.

Johnny thought about it. He very much doubted that there had been any misunderstanding, and he could see that Ross might take the two old men very seriously after what he, Johnny, had told him the police already knew. Still. "Maybe," he said.

"Have a little more bourbon, son." The congressman pushed the bottle closer. "You know what an ugly big son of a bitch Ben is. And he was carrying his rifle. We were going varmint-shooting, he explained to Ross."

"We," Johnny said.

"Well," the congressman said, "I had a rifle, too. You know how it is, son. Sometimes two shooting varmints are better than one."

"I see," Johnny said.

"We told Ross that we stopped by because we'd heard that twenty-five sections of land adjoining Ben's ranch were for sale, and that we figured we could whomp up a local syndicate to take over the property, sort of keep it in the family, so to speak." He smiled again. "The trouble with Eastern dudes buying land out here sight unseen, we explained, was that sometimes there were problems maybe they didn't quite know how to cope with."

"But you do," Johnny said. His face and his voice were expressionless.

"Son," Mark Hawley said, "Ben and I have been around here a long time. There aren't many things that crop up we haven't dealt with before." He paused. He smiled. "Times change. Remember that. But sometimes the old remedies still do the trick. How about another small spot of bourbon?"